A Heart Condemned to Roam

BRIAN CARMODY

Black Rose Writing | Texas

First printing

This is a work of fiction. Names, characters, businesses, places, events, and incidents are either the products of the author's imagination or used in a fictitious manner. Any resemblance to actual persons, living or dead, or actual events is purely coincidental.

ISBN: 978-1-68433-468-1
PUBLISHED BY BLACK ROSE WRITING
www.blackrosewriting.com

Printed in the United States of America
Suggested Retail Price (SRP) $16.95

A Heart Condemned to Roam is printed in Chaparral Pro

*As a planet-friendly publisher, Black Rose Writing does its best to eliminate unnecessary waste to reduce paper usage and energy costs, while never compromising the reading experience. As a result, the final word count vs. page count may not meet common expectations.

Editor: Cora Carmody
Cover Art: Daniel Carmody

*To every woman I have every loved, and everyone
who has ever told me the meaning of life.*

SPECIAL THANKS

Once again to God, through whom all things are possible.

To my mother and father, Colonel Kevin and Cora Carmody, who have done more for me than I could ever repay.

All the real people who have inspired this story, these characters, and their lessons, whether they know it or not.

Chris Isaak, Serenader of *Dreamland*. Thank you for the music.

Gordon Jackson, for naming Tiebreaker.

Christy Burnett and Ron Friedman for all your praise and support.

To America itself, as character and inspiration.

To *Black Rose Writing* for another opportunity.

And finally, you, the reader. Thanks for everything!

A Heart Condemned to Roam

All my life, people have been telling me the meaning of life....

I stand here by the side of the road, leaning against my beat-up truck somewhere in the middle of the desert. It's a stark, silent landscape, a wide-open world and plenty of fluffy clouds in the wild blue sky. I stare into the empty distance, contemplating, and thinking about all the things everyone has tried to tell me.

MOTHER

I remember my Mother, a wise, ethereal beauty, playing with me in the grass when I was two or three years old. It is my first memory. She is holding up my arms to help me walk. Maybe I can already walk on my own. Maybe she is just playing. We sit down on the cool grass, and she points up at the sky.

"He made the sky, He made the trees. He made the birds, and He made the bees. He made you and He made me. Do you know how? Ben? Do you know how God did that?"

"How?" I ask, not even knowing what the question meant.

"With love." Her voice is so soft and warm, as only a mother's can be. This is how I remember her. "God does everything with love, because love is all there is. That's all you ever have to remember, Ben."

OUR FATHER

...who art in Heaven, hallowed be thy name. Thy kingdom come, thy will be done, on Earth as it is in Heaven. Give us this day our daily bread and forgive us our trespasses as we forgive those who trespass against us. Lead us not into temptation, but deliver us from evil. In the name of the Father, and the Son, and the Holy Spirit, amen.

THE PLEDGE OF ALLEGIANCE

I pledge allegiance, to the flag, of the United States of America. And to the republic, for which it stands, one nation under God, indivisible, with liberty and justice for all.

MR. TODD

I am in Kindergarten

Mr. Todd is the first black grown-up I know. In 1990s Northern Virginia, we aren't yet saying African-American. Kevin Furley is the only black kid in my class, and Mr. Todd is the only black teacher at Oak Hill Elementary. He is a tall, wide-eyed man with a deep, sonorous voice. He reads to us *The Car in the Hat Comes Back*. He draws a picture of the cat on the chalkboard where the cat took off his hat, revealing a smaller cat underneath. He tells us what that means, brings up an old riddle and ties it to the universe.

"This is infinity. Maybe you don't know what that means yet. But it's very, very big. It goes on forever."

He draws a sideways figure eight. I do not know the significance yet, just that it is immense, and it is important.

"When The Cat came back, he took off his Hat, revealing a smaller Cat, with a smaller Hat, but that selfsame trick. And those smaller contain more and more, onward and onward into infinitesimal infinity, until the size, and the portion becomes a quantum so elemental it subsumes the nature of the universe and becomes something less, and more, than the very grounding of creation itself. And it is at that point you realize that it is not what's under the hats that eternally shrink and recur that matters, only that still they do so, as the continuing and self-sustaining microproof, warrant and meaning...Of an existence without end."

I think Mr. Todd had wanted to be a physicist at one point. Or a philosopher, like everyone in this story. What he is saying is lost on us, but it stays with me. I think there is something here.

THE BOY SCOUT OATH

On my honor, I will do my best to do my duty to God and my country and to obey the Scout Law. To help other people at all times; to keep myself physically strong, mentally awake, and morally straight.

SCHOLASTIC APTITUDE TEST.

I am in high school. Mrs. Marley, a humorless but kind woman, passes out the SATs. I look over mine with a tremendous amount of apprehension.

Mrs. Marley stands at the front of the class, holding up one of the test booklets. She is deadly serious as she addresses us.

"Ladies and gentlemen, not to belabor the point, nor do I wish to come off as melodramatic, but it is no hyperbole that this test is the singular most important moment of your young lives thus far. What this is not, is a simple test. This is a crossroads that will determine what school you get into, what path you will be on for the rest of your existence. THIS is your life."

She is only saying what I have felt in my guts for months. My stomach is a pit of cold emptiness. This is the test.

I am still in the desert. I am sitting in the booth of a truck stop diner. I look out at the clouds, white puffs in an endless blue sea. Those clouds are like a dream to me. I remember when I binged *The X-Files* with Winona. There was an episode called "Dreamland". More than the episode itself, the title stayed with me.

Dreamland. I repeat that to myself, because it just seems to fit where my mind's at, where I'm at. Sitting in my car or in this booth, feeling the minutes pass by like clouds floating through the way. I feel a strange sense of serenity as I face the past and think of the ever ebbing white. In a musical coincidence, a leitmotif of life, the diner's radio starts to play one of the songs from one of the CDs I brought on this trip. My ears perk up, and I smile, though it is not a smiling song, and I fade into it. Chris Isaak. *The Best of Chris Isaak.* Winona used to say that Greatest Hits compilations are the most unrefined form of music, but maybe I'm just lazy that way. Pedestrian. A listener who appreciates what makes him feel without ever being a connoisseur.

It's a big, blue, Spanish sky. Lay on my back and watch clouds roll by.

Chris speaks to me. I dub him the Serenader of Dreamland and place him in those soft clouds. I sink into his sonorous, haunting voice, soft yet masculine as it weaves tales, some jaunty, some melancholy, of love and sorrow. It's the latter I feel right now. The cover of this album, as basic as some might find its existence, stays with me. He's a silhouette, a standing shadow. You can't see his gentle blue eye as he waits, head lowered and body pensive with the Golden Gate Bridge in the background, the sun receding in that sad twilight hour between night and day. This music is, in this moment, the soundtrack to my soul. Even the photo is forlorn.

I got time to wonder why she left me.

Empty land all around. Down the road, a billboard. On a yellow background, cartoonish blue letters. "WHAT IS THE THING? 500 MILES". The highway is littered with such billboards. It is what my father would refer to, less than charitably but not necessarily inaccurately, as a "tourist trap". I loved them. House of Mirrors. Ripley's Believe it Or Not. Even today, I'm hooked by that question mark.

It's a slow, sad Spanish song. I knew the words, but I sang them wrong.

My mind is in other times and places.

The one I love has left and gone without me.

My memories are in fragments. I play them back and forth, but not in order, like a CD of life's greatest hits that keeps skipping around.

Now she's goooooone, our world has changed, watching a blue sky, thinking of rain...

FIRST CLASS

It is the first class of the new term. Professor Wilkinson, a stout man, whose sometimes pompous attitude belies his engaging warmth, gives his class a lecture on extinction.

I know him very well. He is my mentor. He is the end all be all for my academic career. I don't always understand what he says, let alone approve or endorse, but I owe so much to him, and he is always worth listening to.

"Death!" He gets our attention, making his point. "Death. Decay. Erosion. Entropy. Extinction."

He pauses before his massive class, which includes me. I am now in college.

"Not the lightest of topics, I admit."

He smiles. We laugh. I nod.

"But surely the most vital. After all, aren't we all- every single one of us- going to die?"

Then I notice her, sitting right in front of me. Winona. She is an artsy, Goth girl. She doodles in her notebook.

"Whether today, next week or 80 years from now, your heart will cease to beat, and you will cease to exist. You're young. Some of you probably think you're immortal."

Pratt, a wise-aleck in the front row, points to himself. "Yo!"

Wilkinson gives a benevolent chuckle. "Yes. Well, you may like to think so, Mr. Pratt. But history is full of men and women who made the same claim- with less irony and more bloodshed. Caligula, Genghis Khan, Countess Elizabeth Bathory- basically, the worst humanity has to offer. But they too learned that no one lasts forever, that death is inevitable, intrinsic and undeniable."

Winona knows she has caught my attention. She turns around and smiles, holding up her latest doodle- a sketch of Wilkinson with a black hood and a sickle held by a bone hand. "DEATH!" he says.

I chuckle. She likes that.

"And even if you should wish to believe in an afterlife- some sort of world yet to come- every religion acknowledges that to get there- you must leave here. No one gets out of this world alive."

Holden, my friend directly to my right (in every way), a tall, muscular guy with a buzz cut and an inscrutable temperament, nudged me. "Hank Williams up there never heard of Enoch?"

I nod. Fair point.

"Well, to summarize, this is not going to be a cheery course. But nor is this an indulgence in nihilism. No, I think you're find that the road to comprehending the universe is rarely a primrose path, there are no easy answers..."

I stand up and make my way down the steps toward the front. I finish his thought. "And X NEVER marks the spot."

I make eye contact with Winona. She smiles.

"Well put," he says graciously, putting his hand on my shoulder. "Ben Carter will be my teaching assistant this semester. You can direct all minor queries toward him."

Winona speaks up, wryly. "What's the meaning of life?"

I'm already infatuated. "Yeah, well, that'll be on the final." I try to sound casual.

Holden grins. The class shuffles out.

Before we can depart, Wilkinson makes his final appeal of the day.

"And by the way, if you want to get more perspective on your own insignificance, I suggest checking out the Museum of Natural History, for their glib but grandiosely titled exhibition 'The History of The Cosmos, Part I'. Do see your beloved TA for how this can translate into extra credit!"

That night, Holden and I are sitting in a booth in the back of Danny's Bar. It is a "college bar", a term I still don't understand, as the majority of underclassmen are underage. Holden and I are "over-classmen", a term he coined and proudly bandies about with the tone of "uber-mensch".

Holden downs two tequila shots. "Do you think that man would be so flippant on the subject of death had he ever killed a man?" With Holden, who is always certain, a question is always a statement.

I keep in mind that Holden does know a thing or two about that. "Uh...hard to say."

He goes on. "That's the problem with these liberal literati. Intellectual elites. Armchair nihilists. They're all talk. Everything is theory, it's all academic. Let me tell you, in that instant when you've got a wave of shrapnel flying towards your face at the speed of sound...You're not thinking about your dissertation."

"Well, maybe he's known someone who's died."

"We all have dead people in our families. This alone is unexceptional. But to take a life. Ah! That is..."

But he sees that my attention is elsewhere.

There she is, at the bar. Standing with her friend Ayishah. Winona, never regarding the rules, lights up a cigarette, as if it's the most natural thing in the world.

Holden is amused. "Oh, but a young man's thoughts turn to fancy."

Winona is admonished by the bartender.

"What?" I'm uselessly defensive. "Who's fancy? I'm not a fancy boy."

Winona rolls her eyes as she extinguishes her smoke.

Holden is adamant. "Go up and talk to her. Do it now."

She saw me from across the bar. Quickly, too quickly, I break off eye contact.

"I don't know, Holden..." I try not to sound hopeless.

She quickly orders another beer.

My friend is impatient. "You craven little boy." But his tone, while chiding, is supportive, and reads harsher than it sounds. "If I can withstand an onslaught of insurgent fire, you can at least strike up a conversation with a member of the fairer sex."

"Well when you put it that way..."

A miracle. She is walking over. My heart palpitates. My mind races with a thousand scenarios. I was not prepared for this. I try to check my excitement. Surely she is walking in this general direction, and not at myself specifically.

"Hey-oh! TA!"

I wave as she walks over.

Holden looks at me, surprised. Surprised more than I am, even. "It appears the lady has taken her own druthers."

"Stop." I can't let her hear that.

She reaches our booth. She sits down and puts the beer on the table.

Holden mocks annoyed. "So yeah, just sit on down."

She ignores him. She wants to talk to me. "Ben, right?"

"Correct on both counts. Ben Carter, Teaching Assistant for Professor Mark Wilkinson's course 'Existential Entropy: The Ultimate Extinction of Sentient Beings'."

She is impressed. "Quite an introduction."

It was, but my self-consciousness at being too verbose or self-laudatory passes. She is welcoming.

Holden one-ups me, as is his wont. "Mine is more distinguished. First Lieutenant Holden McQueen, United States Marine Corps."

"Wow. That's awesome. I'm Winona Helmsley, if you check your roster." If for a moment I felt threatened by my friend, she says, "and this is for you."

She slides the beer to me. I am surprised. I take the cold perspiring beverage, brushing her warm fingers in the process.

"Oh. Wow. Thank you." I can't get over this. "Why?"

"Eh, you looked a little dry. Also, you didn't currently have a beverage."

Holden stands up to recuse himself. "Excuse me kids. I must to the facilities." God Bless him.

He pats me on the shoulder and walks off. Winona salutes and I follow suit, though I am not sure how sincere she is.

"Was he really in the Marines?"

"It's not just a haircut. He's actually still in the Reserves. Might reenlist after he graduates."

"Why would he do that?"

"I don't know." And I don't want to talk about Holden. I still think he's more interesting than me, and certainly manlier. "Hey, I saw that little sketch you drew- Of the Professor as The Grim Reaper."

"I should hope so. I was holding it right in your face," she teases. "You're not going to tattle on me, are you?" Everything about her is precious.

"Nah, I'm cool like that. Just pretty funny. Artistic. And with a very short turnaround time, I must say."

"Yeah, I'm cool like that. I don't know- I mean, he's your guy, and I'm sure you love him and all- but a bit pompous, bit pretentious, a bit doom and gloom, don't you think?"

"More than a bit. No, I totally agree. A man definitely suited to caricature."

"Oh we all are. Every single...what was it, 'conscious entity'?"

"Sentient Being."

"Everyone's a caricature in their own fashion. McCaulfield back there is definitely getting the Winona Treatment."

"He- He hates Catcher in the Rye."

She figures. "Marine getting his Master's? Soldier cum Scholar."

"A warrior poet."

She likes that. She playfully slaps my arm. "Could have him with a rifle in one hand, and a...murder-board? Matormord?" She shakes her head, frustrated and disappointed. "You know. A graduation cap."

"Oh yeah. I know what you're talking about. I just don't know the word."

"Damnit. I would have sounded a lot smarter if I had gotten that right."

"Probably."

She tries to think of what next to say. "So..."

I break the ice. I am about to make my proposal, to ask a girl out, something I have very little experience doing. I speed through it and feign confidence. "I know what you're thinking, and the answer is yes. I would be happy to accompany you through the History of the Cosmos."

"That might take a while."

"I've been there before and am in a position to give you an excellent tour." She smiles.

Ayishah comes over from the bar, impatient. "Winona, let's go!"

Winona gets up. "Catch you soon. And we ARE going!"

I watch her leave.

As does Holden as she comes back.

"She bought me a beer," I say simply.

Holden nods as he sits down, looking at said beer. He appreciates the significance.

"'First time a woman's done that.'" I quote Jon Osterman. Billy Crudup in the movie.

"You should celebrate," he gestures. "Have a drink."

"No, it's from *Watchmen*. When Dr. Manhattan- "He's never had patience for this reference. "I. Do Not Care. About *Watchmen*."

I watch her stop at the door. She smiles and waves warmly.

Leaving me thinking. Effervescent. What to make of that? "It's just so odd. So..."

•   •   •   •   •

"...special." It was so special, I think as the alarm clock wakes me up from a haze of that fond recollection.

I stare up at the ceiling in the blue hours of morning. Melancholy.

I am just coming out of that early morning haze between sleep and wake. I was harping on a memory, not of my own experience, but of a film I saw several years earlier. *Twin Peaks: Fire Walk With Me*. I like Chris Isaak as a singer and actor. His last scene in that film, he sees a beautiful ring on the ground. Then he picks it up, and he disappears. Vanishes into the ether. We don't know find out where he goes. The price of beauty. It's a fate that seems quite poignant now.

I sit on the edge of my bed. I am in the bedroom of my apartment in Santa Monica. It is a modestly sized, moderately priced residence. Rent works differently as a professional in California than a student in Virginia. Being an adult means being practical. Waking up alone, I accept the emptiness of my surroundings. It's quiet, because nobody else is here. Even I, my thoughts drifting, as always, to the past and the future, am hardly here.

I wish to fall back into bed and enter the embrace of some sweet beckoning dream, the dream I felt before I thought of the film, the traces of which I still feel even as content fades away. Was I in the Middle East? Was it a fantasy inspired by the Arabian Nights? Was I Aladdin? Were there bandits or rocs? Was there a princess?

But I have a job to get to, so I get up.

I shower.

I get dressed. I go through my ties. I see one with a Rubik's Cube theme. I crack a smile.

Now dressed and wearing the Rubik's Cube tie, I come into the kitchen. Pour myself a cup of coffee. Swiss Hazelnut. Instant. My father says I should get one of those little machines that brews it for you, but I don't feel the need. It's just so easy to stir a spoon into a cup. It's only coffee.

I see yesterday's mail on the counter. I hadn't bothered to check it.

I go through the mail. Nothing interesting. Until...

I'm so startled I drop the letter.

It's a black envelope with white calligraphy for the address, written in a very familiar handwriting.

I pick the letter up and look at it with awe. I can't believe it.

Ever so carefully, I open the envelope. I hold the letter to my nose and breathe in deeply, as if I could detect her scent.

My lip trembles and my hand shakes ever so slightly as I read.

Ben...

NATURAL HISTORY

I stand in front of a massive wall mural. The history of the universe, illustrated timeline, scaled, from the Big Bang to the Year of our Lord 2013. All of human history, from the Cro-Magnon era to last week's So You Think You Can Dance, only encompasses the last half an inch or so.

We are at the Smithsonian's National Museum of Natural History.

I stand back from the wall, taking it in, contemplating the notion of my own insignificance.

"Where are you Ben?"

I do not look back at Winona as she walks up to stand next to me.

"When. When am I?"

She squints one eye and puts her finger at the end of the line. "Right...about...there- then."

I try to correct her. "No, I think that would be about the Renaissance."

"Well, I guess it really doesn't matter. That's the point, isn't it? All of human history is just a pinpoint in the grand scheme of things. We just...haven't been here very long," she finishes plainly.

I take out my phone and look at it. "About half an hour."

Winona strolls along, taking in the huge mural. "It's very *Vertigo*, you know?"

She moves two fingers along the timeline and talks in a distant, ethereal voice, like Kim Novak in Vertigo. "Here I died...Here I was born...it was just a blink of the eye to you."

I look at where her fingers are. "You were born sometime in the Paleozoic Era?"

Winona stands up straight. She takes a serious, grand tone. Like a goddess. "Behold. I am an ancient being from a distant epoch and I am immortal and terrible and great."

I observe her appreciatively. "You're some kind of being."

We go through the museum, observing his exhibits. Ancient beings from distant epochs that are, no doubt, terrible and great, but clearly not immortal, and never as beautiful as she.

We stop before a glass display case. A sabertooth tiger statue.

With Winona, I'm not afraid to say what I think. "Now this reminds me of Batman: The Animated Series."

She instantly knows where I am going with a perfect synchronic chemistry. "YES".

"Catwoman- or I guess, Selina Kline was at a museum or an endangered species fundraiser or something.

I smiled incredulously. It really was too much.

"'Extinction'," Winona quoted. "She was comparing us...to them."

"Yeah."

"But this is a stuffed animal. It's not extinct because it never was." She turns around, points across the room. "That's real."

We walk over. A display of a human skeleton from the Paleolithic Age. Next to the display is an artist's rendition of what this prehistoric woman might have looked like. In the illustration she is clad in primitive garb and carrying her baby across a field.

"Those are bones," she says, hopelessly poignant. "She was a real person."

Winona puts her hand on the glass. Reaching out to touch this person she never knew. "What did you think her life was like?"

I try to picture it. The Prehistoric Woman walking across the open field, holding her baby. Hunger and danger are constant companions. And always, the unknown. All of human history before her. She didn't have any conception that one day she'd be behind a glass wall in a museum as we watched. She just lived her simple, short life.

We look at the woman in silent contemplation.

Winona eventually breaks it. "Kyle."

"What?"

"Selina Kyle."

We walk around the outside of the museum, in the park. It is a cloudy, gray day, given to such pondering.

Winona is pondering. "I guess it's supposed to put things in perspective, right? I mean, that was Wilkinson's point, wasn't it?"

I agree. "Insignificance."

"I don't buy that. If we can even think that, it's got to mean something right? I mean, if we can conceive of the concept of insignificance, isn't that significant? I think, therefore I am...important."

I venture into the religious. I share. I have to share this part of myself with her. Otherwise, what's the point? "We're children of God. How can any of us not matter?"

She accepts it. Doesn't raise an eyebrow. "So, this universal stuff doesn't freak you out?"

"Oh, it terrifies me. And depresses me." I open up. "I compiled a list of the Four Most Depressing Things that I could think of."

"That's weird." But not in a cruel way. She's curious.

I am not nervous about telling her. Not too nervous. "Not really. I mean, it's just a philosophical summation-"

"-No, I mean having four. Why not ten or five or just the one?"

"They have varied subjects," I explained. "One cosmological, one medical, one, erm, sexual-" I stumble, "and one religious."

She smirks. "And what is the most depressing *sexual* thing you can think of?"

Is my face red? I try not to imagine. "Uh not, not on a, the first, uh..."

"Date?" She terrifies me, in the most wonderful way I have ever known.

I dodge that one. I see a statue. Some kind of memorial. A Confederate General, a man who, like the Prehistoric Woman before him, would never have dreamt what role he would play, as discussion or distraction, in our modern-day drama. "I love this one."

Before I can walk over, she puts her hand on my arm. Warm and soft. Stopping me. Eye contact. Smiles affectionately. "Hey..." She lets it linger. It is alluring, terrifying.

I awkwardly return her smile. "Hey."

She removes her arm and we continue walking. I wonder what it was I missed.

I clear my throat. "Well, how about you pick a different depressing subject?"

"Oh...How about...Cosmological?"

"The Heat Death of The Universe."

"Heavy."

"I'm not an astrophysicist. Professor Wilkinson's class is philosophy. But I think about things."

"Don't we all?"

I laugh it down. "There are several secular theories for the end of the universe. Big Rip, Big Crunch...A lot of people like the idea of an infinite restart button, eternal return and all that."

"Oh, being IS so unbearably light, isn't it?"

Glad she gets the reference. "Maybe. But I think the latest prevailing theory has scientists denying the idea that we are nailed to eternity like Christ to the cross. The most popular theory currently is-"

"-Heat Death. Got it. That's where everything just shuts down, right?"

"The stars burn out. No new matter. No energy left. Entropy cannot be reversed. But there's no new Big Bang, no cataclysmic event to cap everything off. It's just nothing happening anymore...ever again. A cold, empty void. Forever."

She let that sink in, and responded with the succinct, contemporary, but utterly appropriate "Bummer."

"And it scares me. It scares me to tears some nights. Because if the universe lasts billions...trillions...illions of years, but then just fades away. *Forever*. Because if that is what happens, then the entirety of EVERYTHING that ever existed or ever will exist is swallowed up by an empty eternity. Everything is pointless."

She coos sympathetically "No, don't say that."

"I don't like to."

"Is that why you believe in God?"

"I'm not sure it is a choice. Although I do admit that theological voluntarism has enormous appeal to me.

"What's that?"

"I Want to Believe."

I had told her all about it, and why it depressed me, and she was more intrigued than weirded out.

I notice where we were. I still didn't own a car, and we had reached my bus stop. All good things...

"This is my bus stop. This was nice." Seal the deal for a second date, Ben. "I look forward to-"

"Aren't you going to walk me back to my car? I can give you a ride back here?"

What was that? I am puzzled, but receptive. I cherish any opportunity to spend more time with her, even if it makes so little sense.

I buckle up. "I'm sorry Holden couldn't make it."

"No you're not."

"No I'm not."

Winona is now starting the car. The air is electric with some unknown anticipation. Is it a lingering reluctance to end this encounter? No, she has something more Earth-shattering in mind.

She looks down, coy. What is in her head?

After a moment, she turns to me and offers one of the best moments of my young life.

"Hey, do you mind if I kiss you?"

Hey.

Hey, do you mind?

Hey, do you mind if I kiss you?

Kiss you.

KISS.

YOU.

I will never forget that line, as long as I exist. Perhaps even more than that immortal moment that came next. It stayed with me, as something significant, something powerful, something *real*. It was happening to me.

I was stunned, but more than welcome.

"No."

In an instant, our mouths have come together. And it lasts more than a good long moment.

Her cool, soft lips pressing against mine. Her wet tongue caressing mine. Her face is so close. Everything is a flash of sensual experience. I can't see. I simply am. We are.

I don't know how it stops, who breaks it off, but eventually it ends, and she starts the car.

I sit there in silence, trying to process what just happened.

I open my mouth, about to say "Thank you", but quickly decide that would be inappropriate. This is not a gift. This is not a favor. This is her. This simply *is*.

Winona gets to my stop. She is casual, as if she did not just move worlds. She smiles. "So I'll see you in class? I mean, 'cause class is tomorrow. But we should hang out again soon."

"Yeah! Definitely."

I unbuckle and open the door.

"Bye!" she waves.

"Bye."

•　　•　　•　　•　　•

She drives away. I try to sort out what just happened. My mind is blown. From now on, there would be before and after. I felt a twinge of melancholy that it has taken until my twenty-third year, and that this age group being what it is, my first kiss must necessarily be French. If it had happened when I was 12, would it be just the lips, more chaste, and innocent? But why dwell on that? This is one of the high points of my life, and always will be. Nor is the romance cheapened by the swelling of my pants. I wait for my bus, overwhelmed by the inexhaustible beauty of life and the surprise of joy.

DAD

The gentle hum of the fluorescent lights underscore my mix of emotions as I sit in my cubicle. I am wearing my Rubik's Cube tie, and Winona's letter is on my desk.

This is a very clean and well-lit office building in Santa Monica. I did not anticipate a career writing copy for the Carter and Stone advertising firm. Life takes us funny places. But they're not always funny. Sometimes they're just sad.

The banality of an uneventful morning is broken when Dad walks up. He smiles at me.

"Hey, Dad."

Jovial as usual. "Working hard or hardly working?"

"Seriously?" That line's so stale, no matter how ironically he meant to use it "How's the day?"

How to answer that? "Significant?"

He's puzzled, curious. "Good significant, or...significant?"

I reach for the letter. Stop. "Hard to say."

Dad sighs. "Bit dull around here though, you noticed?" He leans in. "What do you say we play hooky? Cut out early, take Stacey out on the marina?"

"Well."

"We can talk about all things significant, and everything in between."

•　　•　　•　　•　　•

Dad and I are out on *STACEY*, a beautiful long sailboat, out in the Santa Monica waters on a lovely day. It really is. I smile, despite everything.

Dad steers. "Ah, ebb and flow. That Santa Monica chop. You gotta watch out for her, but boy does she give you some rhythm!"

I look into the surf. Dad notices that I am currently disinterested in matters nautical.

"You wanna take the helm for a bit here, Gilligan?"

"Winona's back." I say this enormous fact plainly, but I don't want to weigh his boat down, so I add, "Skipper."

Dad takes a break from steering the boat and turns back to me. "Oh."

"Not now. She gets back to George Mason in about a month."

He doesn't know what to say, because he doesn't know how I feel. Because I don't know how I feel. "So that's the...significant."

What can I tell him? "I mean, after everything that happened...or...didn't-" He doesn't know that and doesn't have to, "...between us...She hurt me, Dad. She really hurt me bad."

"But now she's coming back."

"I don't know how I'm supposed to feel about that. I mean, part of me wants to just drop everything and go to her. But then part of me thinks I should just throw the letter into the trash, be done with it." I look over the edge. "Maybe I should have brought it."

But I don't know.

Dad nods. This is hard for him. He's not an overtly sentimental man. Affability is his wheelhouse, and direct catharsis comes not as easily. "I ever tell you what happened between me and your mother? I mean the truth, not some sanitized feel good bull."

Sinking feeling in my stomach. I don't want to bring this all up. "Dad, you don't have to..."

He shakes his head. He thinks of the boats, and the people in them, and he relates in nautical terms what he knows of humans.

"After a certain point you realize, it's not what you think you care about that matters, it's the big things you willfully choose to ignore. People, people are small. We don't get along. We bump into each other, like boats in the current, going opposite directions, but all in the same river. And these little collisions, they last. Believe me, they last. You're frustrated with the other boat's captain, or just the other guy rowing in a little boat just like yours-and most are, trust me. We're small and the same. You curse him out for bumping into you, swear a little that he scuffed up your hull. But you scuffed up his too. It's impossible and unimportant to assign blame, because it's just the way the current brought you together. Don't ignore that, never ignore that. You collided for a reason. And though you may shake your head and swear off this brief annoyance five minutes later, there will come a time, maybe tomorrow, maybe in 40 years, when your boat is rocking in the stockyard, when you realize that that man you bumped into was just like you, another captain on the same sea, trying to find his way home. It was a genuine human interaction, a chance to make a new friend, discover something new about yourself, and you wasted it, both of you wasted it, arguing about whose fault it was that you met in the first place. Don't. Don't. Take every opportunity you can find, even the bad ones, as a chance to find a fellow human being. Because we're all on this river together, even if we're in different boats. I just wish I had known that at the time." In unknowing wisdom, the familiar pain. "I'm sorry. I'm- I'm sorry."

After a long silent moment, I try to take it in. "So you're saying..."

He is firm. "Go to her. Find your path and find out where it takes you."

•   •   •   •   •

I am still in the diner. Memory in fragments and all that.

I poke at my meal, scrambled eggs (runny) and sausage (greasy) half-eaten. I nurse a cup of black coffee (weak) and gather my thoughts. This is a small town, little more than a truck stop, really. As I drive through, as I often do on road trips, I look at the little houses on the side of the highway, and I wonder.

Who are these people? What do they do? What kind of life do you think they have built in the middle of nowhere?

If they have kids, and some of them must, what kind of childhood is that? Nearest school must be ten miles away. Who do they play with?

I feel sad, because it must be a terribly lonely existence. What's Friday's entertainment? Biking down to the gas station for an Icee and a couple of rounds on the arcade game?

I'm condescending. I don't know these people. I know nothing about them, who they are, or how they live. Maybe they love it. Maybe it's simple out here, uncomplicated. Maybe they're blessed with all the stars in the sky we can't see back in the city. Maybe they like things without so many people and so much chatter all around. Maybe they make quick friends, passersby like me, who drive though on our way from one place to another.

There's something innately human about that, and I find it more than a little poignant. Dad was right. We're all just floating around, on our own boats or in our own cars. We take our own paths, every single one of us, and sometimes we bump into each other. I don't think anybody really knows where they're going. Not really.

"Do you want some more coffee?"

Leroy, his red tag reads. I wonder if he would be offended if he knew what I was thinking, what questions I wasn't ever going to ask. I wonder what he thought of me. Probably that I was a businessman on a trip or something. Or a college student going off to meet some buddies. We all make assumptions.

"I'm good." He turns to leave, then I think better. "Actually, yeah, I'll have a fill up."

He fills my cup to the brim. "You coming off the interstate?"

"Yup. I just passed through Arizona."

He raises his eyebrows suggestively. "You see The Thing?"

"I saw the billboards."

"Yeah, there are a lot of them."

"No, I didn't go in. What is it?"

"That's a secret, chief." He winks and goes along his way.

Well was it a jackalope or something, chief? Bottomless pit? Flying Saucer to rival Roswell? I regret not taking that stop, even though I would have lost a couple of hours. But what are a couple of hours when you uncover one of the great secrets of the universe? What if Lewis and Clark were so eager to get there on time?

"Chief". Leroy looks like a Native American. I wonder how he got that name. I wonder what his ancestors did. I wonder if they ever imagined their descendent cracking wise and serving coffee to a truck stop tourist like me. But whatever. He isn't complaining. And he has a whole life, I'm assuming, outside of being an Apache. Maybe he has a pickup truck and a girlfriend who wears a jean jacket. Maybe they drive up to "The Point", wherever that was, and sit on his hood. Maybe he tells her sweet things, telling her he loves her, he'll always be with her, and one day, someday soon, he's going to take her out of this one-horse town, because she deserves something more.

Or maybe they're happy just where they are.

But I go on.

I take out a map of the USA and put it on the table. My course is a parabola of the country. Los Angeles bell curving up through Kansas to Chicago, then down from Chicago to Tennessee, and finally up to Virginia. I nod at my route, satisfied.

I take out a black felt tip pen and start to doodle on my napkin. A skull-faced gargoyle. Like a less talented attempt at...

A BRIEF HISTORY OF HUMAN DEPRAVITY

...The monstrosities in Winona's notebook. She takes a break from sketching ghosts and goblins and the like, to appreciate her surroundings.

We are in a booth at Fuddruckers, great family novelty burger chain. Americana on the wall, huge juke box, you name it.

"I love this place," she tells me. "It's got nostalgia, you know?"

I agreed. "World's Greatest Hamburgers."

"Used to come in here all the time with my parents."

I look through her notebook. At all her creepy drawings. Pale Victorian children with large eyes and sallow cheeks. A spider lady whose hair curled up into webs of frayed iron. A ghostly parade of amputees, headless torsos, and things that shouldn't be.

"These are really nice, you know? Very...Burtoneseque."

"Very predictable assessment. I wasn't born in Hot Topic yesterday, you know." She's not offended. She's amused. She wants me to ask.

"Try me. What are your real influences?"

"Edward Gorey's a big one. I could see myself drawing like him. Victorian era Gothica in general. And Charles Addams. He's creepy, but in a kid way, you know?"

She lights up a cigarette. Looks down. Contemplates.

"When you're a kid, monsters come in all shapes and sizes. It could be a thing in your closet with sharp teeth and a lot of red eyes, or just a ghost branch scraping against your bedroom window. But it was all so simple back then. There was an innocence to our fear. What scares us now is more frightening, and a lot more real. It's not the boogeyman that keeps me up at night. It's bills to pay, my Mom's health, and all those shootings. Are we going to go to war, will I get the job, is he even going to call me back, am I doing the right thing? What am I doing with my life, and what happens after death? The oppressively terrifying existential questions about the universe don't come in such easy packages." As a succinct summary, she finished, "I miss my monsters."

It was so sad and true. She had articulated something so many of us must have been aware of all along. She put it into words.

I reach across the table and put my hand on hers. I can't summon monsters, and maybe she didn't want me to. But I could tell her that maybe there were some things she didn't have to be afraid of.

"I'll call you back. I'll always call you back."

She smiles.

Our server, a humorless girl named Gabrielle with a lip ring, comes over in response to Winona's smoking.

"Seriously? Like, for real?"

Winona shrugs. "I guess not."

In a (romantic?) gesture, I take the cigarette from Winona and throw it in my own glass.

"She was only holding it for me."

Gabrielle is not impressed. "I'll give you guys more time."

Winona looks from the retreating waitress to the cigarette floating in my water.

"Well that was a rather pointless sacrifice."

Gallantry isn't dead? "Yeah, I don't know why I did that."

She's curious and reveals some vulnerability. "Do you mind that I smoke?"

"No! In fact, I..." Don't go there, Ben. What were you thinking? Correct. "I mean, it's none of my business."

Pensive. "No. There's more to it than that." She raises an eyebrow. "Go on. What were you going to say?" She can read me, which is intimidating, but she wants to read me, which is encouraging.

"It's weird." I am very self-conscious. But maybe she's okay to be self-conscious around. "I just...I find it kind of sexy."

She loves that. "Really?" she smirks.

I don't have to answer, because Holden comes in. He looks around. He sees us and smiles. He approaches our booth and addresses the table with a grand aplomb. "Home is the sailor, home from the sea."

"Oh God." Winona is not glad to see him. Perhaps she just finds the soldier's personality unbearable, as his following rant will demonstrate, but I tell myself that it's because she wants me to herself.

"And the hunter, home from the hill," Holden finishes with a grand Stevenson flourish.

I obligingly scoot over as Holden invites himself in.

"Hey Holden."

"Sup," Winona relents.

Gabrielle comes by with another cup of water.

"Thank you," Holden nods at her politely.

"We're gonna need another minute," I tell Gabrielle. She is aggravated, but at least tries to hide it.

"They beheaded another reporter," Holden informs us. "Heathens."

"They did?" I am not surprised. It wasn't the first incident of the year, and it wouldn't be the last.

There is a dark part of me that doesn't mind. I find it all exciting. Any time there is an attack, it gets my blood pumping. I am detached from and engaged by the CNN broadcasts, the online articles, the Twitter feed. It all seems like an action thriller. I can't see the people. It is all spectacle. I eat up the casualty count like points in a game. I try not to tell everyone that the Jihad Johnny videos remind me of the Ben Kingsley Mandarin broadcasts in Iron Man 3. I know I should be mortified, angry, sad. I don't know what endorphins the headline "40 killed in Paris" release in me, but the horrible truth is, it doesn't make me feel bad.

Winona, on the other hand, is as she should be. "Damnit! Why can't we just quit with this shit already? It's the 21st century! I know there's all religion, and history and bullshit, but honestly, war?! Don't they know that never works?"

"Doesn't it, though?" Holden challenges, amused. I can tell, he will enjoy upsetting her. He relishes conversations like these. I have heard his pontification before, but to him, Winona is fresh meat.

She is so frustrated. "Hasn't anybody ever cracked open a history book? JUST STOP!"

Holden is dry, and makes his statement plainly, with a tone that indicates he knows how outrageous his thesis is but doesn't care.

"War is underrated."

I cough, because for Winona's sake I must feign incredulity, shock, and disdain. "Come again?"

Holden grins and puts his cup on the table, with his cards.

"Everyone says that war is bad because they know they're supposed to think war is bad, because the tautological roar of clichés is drummed into their heads ad infinitum. 'Give peace a chance!' 'End to war!' 'No Blood for Oil!'" He smirks. "'Just stop!'"

Winona makes an indignant tone. His tone is certain. He never stutters or questions himself. He is a resolute man who speaks in absolutes with a silver tongue.

"And other meaningless and impotent platitudes, deprived of substance or virtue, repeated by the trite masses so that the chance for intelligent recourse is drowned out as if by the mewling of inane infants."

"Excuse me?!" Winona is not content to be one of those infants.

Mellifluous, he patronizes, without passion, explaining patiently to children who don't have his warrior's wisdom.

"You are excused, Noni, for your notion is not entirely of your own making, but the byproduct of being raised in an environment that subjugates reason for emotion and would choose to mindlessly condemn the sacred institution of war while living in a world crafted by its practice."

I see it as he narrates.

A representative speaks in congress.

Politicians reluctantly speak of war, as the last resort. Why not the first?

I think of all the wars in human history. From the Babylonian invasion of Israel to the War of the Roses to the ISIS of today. It takes the Spanish the better part of 800 years to oust the Moors, but the Anglo-Zanzibar War is over in 45 minutes, without The British Empire suffering a single fatality.

Is there any human endeavor so effective?

Winona is incredulous, outraged.

"Those so-called peacemakers who act so hesitant to trade blows know that ancient and fundamental truth, and that is, for those of us brave, and good enough to survive, the hardships of war are far outweighed by its fruits.

She can't take that. "Its fruits?! What are the benefits of war?!"

"Many, and too numerous to recount all those in the course of human history right now over coffee and crepes, but I shall try. War breeds the survival instinct in man, without which we would have surely perished from the face of the Earth. The very ascension of the human race in the first place is owed entirely to his dominance over smaller, inferior species. The survival of the fittest is nothing if not war on the grandest scale, with results too obvious and absolute to question."

A cave. The Neolithic era. A Cro-Magnon confronts a Neanderthal.

Shall we go back to that very moment when our most ancient ancestors crushed the skulls of the Neanderthal, thus ensuring that we would be the lords and stewards of the Earth?

The cavemen do as he says, the Cro-Magnon bashing the Neanderthal's brains in.

A Cretaceous swamp. A few dinosaurs look up as a massive meteorite descends.

Or further back, when those meager rats survived the massive global attack of a comet so violent as to annihilate all life not worthy to the task?

A little rat or whatever mammal there was at the time, scurries under a rock. Once the fallout is complete, it will emerge from its hole to find there are no more dragons left.

Billions of years ago, bacteria bubbles in the primordial stew.

Cannot life as we know it be attributed to one bacterium quenching its brother?

The Big Bang. Morning. Let There Be Light.

Holden bangs his fist on the table, shaking it and startling us.

"BANG!"

Stars and star stuff and matter and energy expand and explode out from that singularity.

"The origins of the universe itself erupted in a cataclysmic-"

"-Stop!"

Winona tries to take all this in. She's unconvinced but not unimpressed by this speech. She must protest. "Those are all works of nature. A meteorite has no agency. That's hardly a justification for war."

Holden is pleased at the challenge, as he is pleased at all challenges, from all opponents. "You'd have me stick to human affairs. Happily. From even the precepts of civilization, war has been the only constant. Art fades, buildings crumble, gods die, but war, ah war itself remains. The march of progress can be measured in the advancement of war."

He takes out his combat knife. Looks at this instrument of death and survival as he talks.

Brandishing a spear, some ancient hunter wards off a sabretooth.

The spear.

He spears the beast.

The tool that won man's autonomy from the beast, so that the hunted becomes the hunters, lord of this Earth.

A Bronzesmith in Mesopotamia hammers his craft.

Man only started to harness metal…

The Bronzesmith holds up his work. A sword.

A Bronze Age battle. Brutal. The sword doing what it was made for.

…when he found stone did not kill effectively enough.

The Romans ride horses and chariots into battle.

Domestication of the horse and mass production of the wheel were streamlined for their usefulness in battle.

⋅   •   •   •   •   ⋅

I see various empires expand, from the Persian, to the Roman, to the Moorish, Spanish, British Empire.

The spread of civilized human influence came not from diplomacy but by war. We owe all jumps in transportation to such developments.

World War II era scientists plug data into their colossal computer.

Colossus, the world's first digital computer, was developed during, because, and for World War II.

In the Arpanet lab, Vint Cerf and others work on the rudimentary beginnings of...

The internet, your precious network of pornography and lol cats, began as a project for the Department of Defense.

How long have we been here? All of human history, it seems. Holden takes a break to bite his burger. The juice rolls down his chin and he licks it up. He starts up again.

"Make no mistake. War has been at the foreground of every significant technological and social advancement since time immemorial."

"What about all the war crimes?" I finally object.

"War IS a crime!" Winona agrees.

But the advocate is undeterred. "War is the metric, the judgment and the penalty to crimes, and more often than not, justly so. Are there unjust wars and atrocities? Of course! But you condemn those specifically, not a broad, unfocused judgment against the time-tested and holy practice that ends them. The only cure for an unjust war is a righteous one."

Winona is angry, all the more so because she is struggling to argue against the infinite fluidity of his rhetoric. "You're saying killing women and children and destroying countries and committing genocide ends evils?"

He brushes it off. "Certainly. What granted this country its independence? What ended slavery? What brought us out of the Great Depression? What stopped the Holocaust? Every social nicety you appreciate, every moment's peace of mind we owe to the rule of law, an order enforced by men with guns."

"You mean the police?" I ask, "Peace officers?"

"That's only in emergencies!" Winona insists. "Normal people can-everyone should co-exist with morals and love without going to war."

Holden nods. He has an answer for this too. For everything. "Yes. Let us talk about moral virtue, for that is only further to my own point. Every moral construct of right and wrong..."

In Ancient Babylon, a thief has his hand cut off.

...From the time of Hammurabi...

•   •   •   •   •

Perhaps now she is more depressed than angry. Why can't we just laugh at the absurdity? And it must be absurd, surely.

"...Have been understood to carry a weight of punishment, by sword if necessary. Rules without consequence are meaningless, just as freedom without rule is anarchy. That religion is the root of more wars than any other reason is an undeniable fact that makes its adherents uncomfortable, but why should it?"

Christians fight Muslims in The Crusades.

For what greater proof of their deity's grace on Earth, what more tangible evidence, than that he should bless their success in battle...

Conquistadors slaughter Natives in 16th Century South America.

...and give the Christians dominion over the Heathens?

In North Africa, the 7th Century, warriors of the Caliphate fight Moors.

Or extend the Word of The Prophet across the desert?

Holden continues. "The biggest faiths, spread by the sword. Is it any coincidence that the Holy Land is in perpetual unrest, that the three religions overlapping engage in a seemingly endless struggle?"

Winona tries to find common ground. "Those are fanatic, violent zealots. And I agree, organized religion is the problem! War and religion are probably the biggest problems in the world!"

But it is futile. Holden is a man apart. Hoping I won't have to get religious with Winona, I try a cliché. "'War doesn't determine who's right, just who's left.'"

Holden turns to me. "And what greater right there is? What could be more self-evident, more binding a statement of one's agency to exist than the fact that he bested all foes and remained standing to witness?"

"I can't believe I'm hearing this." She hopes. "You're kidding, right? Please tell me you're kidding!"

"Winona, my dear," he responds calmly. He's not trying to condescend. "You profess to be a woman who would bring people together. To unite us."

"With peace! Love!"

"A lofty virtue, to be sure. But peace is that elusive creature seldom earned by the diplomat's hollow words or by holding hands and chanting 'Kumbyah'. More often than not, peace has to be earned- and kept- by the sword. War builds nations. War unites allies under a common banner. War brings people together. War is culture, is technology, is morals, is art. From the dawn of man, war has been the only constant, a fundamental, inexorable part of our species, and if anything about our race is holy, it is war. War is humanity."

And he is done. He has laid down the law immemorial for us mere mortals. His word cannot be challenged or countered. It simply is.

Satisfied, Holden smiles, gets up and wipes his face, before putting his napkin down. Without another word, he walks out of the restaurant, leaving Winona and I to contemplate all...*that*.

She finally finds her speech. "That was seriously messed up."

"I know."

JASON LEE

I drive through West Texas. The Panhandle.

I see him standing by the side of the road, his thumb stuck out. A carefree young good old boy with a green jacket and a slight beard.

I consider, then stop. He needs a ride, and I could use the company. They say you should be careful. He could be dangerous. But he may also be my friend.

He runs up to my side of the car. I roll the window down to his big grin.

"I'm not a serial killer if you're not a homo," he helpfully informs me.

"Fair enough."

$$\bullet \quad \bullet \quad \bullet \quad \bullet \quad \bullet$$

His name is Jason Lee Dauterive. He's a drifter, jack of all trades. Most recently employed as a ranch hand in Nebraska, but he got that itch for the open road. He is crude (but not rude), cocky, opinionated, politically incorrect, talks a lot about sex and assumes you want to hear it all. I like him immediately.

We drive though Texas. Jason Lee is looking at my road map, admiring my travel plan.

"Damn son, but that is one epic road trip."

"Yeah, and it's not just the distance."

He observes the destination. "So what's in DC? Besides museums and Democrats?"

"Northern Virginia. And it's a girl."

He chuckles affably. "It always is." He notes the upward digression. "So what's with the parabola?"

"My sister lives in Chicago. I figure, I might as well see the country, see everyone, on my way to…"

I trail off.

"Tell me about her," he asks eagerly.

"My sister?"

"Nah man. *Her*. All far away and dreamy."

"She's hard to describe."

I think of Winona, dressed in black, full Goth mode, reading a book of Lovecraft in the library.

She was dark…

She glowers theatrically at me.

I remember us at the fair, up in the Italian Trapeze, that magnificent swing ride, with the ecstasy of children we ride high together, hands raised, breathless.

I catch her rapturous smile. It makes me feel light as air.

But she could make you feel so light.

Jason Lee listens appreciatively. "Sounds like a special one."

"She was. The only one."

"Artistic type?"

I smile.

•   •   •   •   •

Happier times. Winona and I sit under a tree in the campus common area. She leans against me as I gently make fun of the sketches in her notebook.

I come across a sketch of an odd superhero, wearing a lot of various colored ties. "Whoa, who's this dweebezoid?"

She laughs. "Shut up! That's Tiebreaker! He's a superhero!"

"I figured. That's why I called him 'zoid. You know, like Freakazoid."

"Oh, I loved that show."

"So what kind of superhero is this Tie-Man?"

"Tie*breaker*. He's the odd kind."

"Any powers?"

Winona sits up, gets totally serious and excited to describe her character. "He can solve a Rubik's Cube. Magically."

"Huh?"

Winona describes it, enthused. "All he has to do is tap on a square, and it'll change colors. Tap enough, change the right ones around, and you've got the whole cube solved. But there is a catch."

I try to follow. "A catch."

She patiently explains. "Each square he taps for the color to change, it requires a tie in the nearby vicinity. So if he's in a room and there's three guys wearing ties, he'll tap three squares, maybe change this one to blue or those two to yellow- but for every square he changes, one of the guys' ties disappears."

I try to comprehend this. Takes me a moment.

"What?!" It doesn't make any sense. There is no connection between...

"Yep."

"So-he- I- wha...So he can solve a Rubik's Cube...by stealing people's ties?"

"Yeah, I don't know how it works. Maybe it's like a matter displacement or something. But just tap, and whoosh! Tie is gone, color is changed."

Where was the rhyme? Where was the reason? It was so wonderfully absurd. "But...what can he do with that power?"

TIEBREAKER

Ruben, aka Tiebreaker, a tall, ordinary-looking man, sits on the couch in his unimpressive apartment. Dressed in ordinary clothes, he works on a Rubik's Cube.

Up until this point, Ruben has led what would ordinarily be considered an unexceptional life. He got decent grades in school, didn't play many sports, and after getting his electrician's license from his local community college, settled in to a stable but less than glamorous job repairing fuse boxes for the city. He is unmarried and lives in a modest but comfortable studio apartment in a building that does not allow dogs, even though he wishes it did.

Ruben does not travel very often, and for the most part stays still, save for Thanksgiving and Christmas, when he goes to visit his sister Ruth and her husband Kevin in Ottawa. Ruben thought about learning French once, even went out and bought a beginner's guide. He soon put it down though, and after finding that one could get around in Canada perfectly fine without speaking any language other than English, he was content to let that be enough.

The city employees Ruben works with regard him as a quiet but friendly man who neither offends nor interests. His supervisor, Lou, likes Ruben, sees him as lonely, and is all too happy to make sure he has every single Thanksgiving and Christmas off, a luxury rarely afforded public utility servants, who must work 365 days a year to keep the lights on for the rest of us. He has a few friends he plays poker with once a month, but mostly he keeps to himself. When he goes on the occasional date, it is pleasant, but sparks rarely fly. Women regard him as fine to look at, but again, not exceptional. People who pass by him on the street pay him no notice at all.

As far as how Ruben views himself, he long ago resigned himself to a quiet ennui that complacency and boredom keep from despair. Thoreau said that the mass of men lead lives of quiet desperation. Ruben picked up *Walden* once, but only got a quarter of the way through. Even so, it is a sentiment that, thus far, has described this man and the way he has existed.

But right now, in this moment, he realizes who he is, what destiny can be, if only he will embrace it.

With great power comes great responsibility. We all know that one. But what about mediocre power? It's not that impressive, I know. In fact, it's pretty weird. And I wouldn't blame you if you didn't see any useful application. But truth be told, there are plenty of people who can change the world without any kind of superpower. Gandhi couldn't magically take off the ties of every mobster in the room. Jesus died a couple thousand years before the Rubik's Cube. I have this gift for a reason, bizarre as it may be. All around me, every day, I see pain. Plenty of pain and plenty of crime. But I see that other thing too. Hope. People are looking for something to believe in, and maybe God sent me to give it to them. A superhero can inspire people, even if he is patently absurd. Ruben Cubert is just a man. To be a symbol, I must become…TIEBREAKER.

I considered. "Mobsters, huh?"

"They wear ties." She made her case. "And how freaked out would they be?!"

I can picture it now. A groom of well-dressed gangsters (all wearing ties, of course), gather around a long table. Mickey Malone, the leader, sits at the head of the table as Even Evan gives a presentation. They are caricatures, of course, the type of mobsters who never existed outside of Dick Tracy. This comic is safe like that.

"So you can see, profits are up 20% across the board. Racketeering especially, which is one of our most lucrative crimes."

Malone is pleased. "Excellent. Excellent. I love crime."

The doors to the board room burst open. In walks Tiebreaker, in all his costumed glory.

"Well y'all better stop the crime," he declares.

The mobsters are shocked, confused, amused.

"Who is this clown?!" Malone demands.

"I'm Tiebreaker." It's a simple declaration of ultimate truth.

"Well you just crashed the wrong party."

Evan approaches Tiebreaker. With lightning fast reflexes, Tiebreaker has whipped out a Rubik's Cube.

Evan is nonplussed. "What is that, one of those multicolored puzzle box whatsitz?"

Tiebreaker taps a green square. It turns blue as Evan's tie instantly vanishes.

"Huh?" Evan doesn't know what just happened.

Sid The Squid is not the only mobster who noticed, and he is quite alarmed. "Evan, your tie!"

Evan looks at his collar and realizes, with horror, that his tie is missing. "What happened?!

"Get him!" Malone shouts. The mobsters get up, try to rush Tiebreaker. Some take out their guns.

But Tiebreaker is too quick for them. His finger is all over his cube, changing the color of the squares and thus removing their ties. This throws off the mobsters so much that all they can do is grip their collars in puzzlement and startlement.

Tiebreaker smiles. The smile of justice.

•　　　•　　　•　　　•　　　•

I am bemused, stunned in the most wonderful way.

"And then they turn themselves in," Winona finishes. Naturally.

"Wow."

"Right?"

"I am without words."

"Most people are."

"That is," I begin, all good-natured, "and I don't think I'm exaggerating here, the most useless, inane, pointless superpower I have ever heard of."

She does not disagree. "I'm not entirely sure I was completely awake when I came up with that.

"Subliminal snooze suggestions. Gotta love it."

She wasn't done with her pitch. "Superman started out in Action Comics. Batman in Detective Comics. Thor in Journey into Mystery."

"Hit me with it."

"Tales of the Inane!"

I kiss her on the forehead. "Never change."

"I don't intend to."

•   •   •   •   •

Jason Lee and I march into the brightly lit, plainly adorned waffle house. We make our way to a booth in the back.

"Hey yo, this is on me, remember," he reminds me.

"Fair enough."

We take our seats. Samantha, the chipper waitress, greets us with a sugary smile.

"Good morning!"

"Good morning yourself." Jason Lee, always the charmer. My simple "Hi" pales in comparison.

"Welcome to the Waffle House! I'm Samantha. I'll be taking care of you this morning.

Jason Lee takes charge. "Samantha, I want you to start us off with two cups of coffee and six waffles to start us off with." Deliberately redundant. Somehow endearing.

"You got it."

"And an ice water." I add.

Jason Lee observes her walking away. "Man, I thought I liked her tits, but I REALLY like her ass."

"Charming." But who was I to talk? I was watching too. At least he was honest about it. "Thanks for ordering for me."

He smirks. "I'm sorry, did you want the Crab Louie? It's the Waffle House, brother."

Fair point. And it was his buck. "Well thanks for paying."

He leans back, cozy. "No trouble, Barney Rubble. Like they say, gas, grass or ass, nobody rides for free. And, having mutually established the No Homo rule, least I can do is throw in for some plaid pancakes.

Well, considering the alternative..."Yes. Much preferable to..."

I trail off as Samantha fills out coffee, then goes to serve other, hopefully less vulgar clientele.

Jason Lee has a wry expression. Here it comes. "But I'm sure you're getting plenty of that on your one epic road trip, am I right?"

"I wouldn't say that, exactly."

But he's not satisfied. "Come on. Come on! You're out here alone, picking plenty of those wild hitchhiker chicks. Lot of strange out there. Lot of strange. I bet you've even gotten road head!" He grins suggestively. "Don't hold out on me Ben. I bet you got some stories!"

Ice cream in hand, Winona and I walk around. She is pleasantly incredulous at my answer.

"Never?"

Not my favorite subject, but I must be honest. "No."

"Not even once?!"

I look down, downplaying it. Answer quickly, quietly. No big deal.

"Nope.

On further contemplation, Winona doesn't find this 100% surprising. She tries to react naturally.

"Cool."

    •   •   •   •   •

The table is full of waffles. I'm full, but Jason Lee continues to shovel it in. We are still talking about carnal matters, though not much has been accomplished or revealed.

"Anyway, it's not really my forte. Nor is this perhaps the best venue for such an explicit conversation."

But Jason Lee is undeterred. "You think anybody cares? This is the Waffle House! This place knows no standards of basic human decency. Abandon all hope ye who enter!"

I laugh a little. "Well when you put it like that."

"I talk about pussy, cause that's what I know and that's what I like. I mean that's it right there! That's all there is. Meaning of life, right between her legs."

There is something so refreshingly juvenile, contagious, in his attitude. He's so carefree, so nonchalant. And the truth is, I *do* want to talk about all the things I never could talk about. But who would listen?

Jason Lee is a rolling stone. He drifts around the country with $300 in his pocket, not knowing where he will be from one night to the next. He is so free. My admiration for him is growing. He is a guy I can have a beer with and tell dirty jokes, with no raised eyebrows, no judgment. The topic is not Christian, but God has sent me a friend I can be completely and totally honest with, and it is a beautiful thing to be cherished.

So I decide to call him on it.

"Okay. So tell me about the clitoris."

Jason Lee is a bit surprised, a bit off put. But he goes for it.

"Alright. What do you want to know? How to find it? How many I diddled? Average size?"

Do I let him in? This is not just sexual, it is philosophical. "It's honestly- it relates- to the most depressing thing I can think of, sexually."

"The clit?" He is confused, but curious. Already he can tell this is not simple bawdy banter, but a genuine and meaningful inquiry.

"You know, I'm not even sure if this is true or not, but I read it in a Kurt Vonnegut book, and he seemed to think he knew everything. I think it was *Breakfast of Champions*."

Jason Lee points to his waffles. "Right here!"

I continue to talk about the book. "He was talking about Dwayne Hoover- that was Bruce Willis in the movie. He said something like, 'Like many men, Dwayne spent too much time on the clitoris.'"

Jason Lee doesn't get it. "Too much time on...the clitoris," he repeats, trying to wrap his head around the problem.

"I think he was saying that- he was critiquing Dwayne Hoover's lovemaking technique on the basis that he was TOO attentive to the clitoris. And that really bummed me out!"

"Why?"

"Well I just always thought- and this isn't from personal experience, of course- I've thought that if you could find...*it*...you'd be in like Flynn. 'All you have to do to please a woman is find the clitoris'. That's what Chef said in *South Park: Bigger, Longer, Uncut*. Freud thought women had two orgasms, the vaginal and the clitoral. He was a nut, but in *The Vagina Monologues* they taught us that the clitoris has "twice, twice, TWICE as many nerve endings as the penis!" So I thought that was it!" I am going a mile a minute, confessing my frustrations at sexual constructs I have no idea about. "But it's not! I mean, I know sex is hard, and you ARE supposed to find it, and spend time on it, but not too much?"

He is invested now. "Ben- ""It's like the movie *Speed*!" I put on a theatrical trailer voice. "If you don't spend enough time on the clitoris she won't come. If you spend too much time- "Thank God, he finally interrupts me. "Ben! Holy shit."

I catch my breath. My nose burns as it does when I feel embarrassed, and I have given far, far too much up. "Sorry."

But he is kind. Patient. Understanding. "First of all, calm down. Jason Lee's going to clear it all up." So genial, so compassionate. Made me wish I had a brother. Although, of course I wouldn't bring up such a subject with anyone I was related to. "You see that guy in the plaid shirt?"

"Where?"

"Two O'clock."

I look to his right, and indeed there is a man in plaid sitting at the counter. Stocky fellow. I'm sure, I hope, he has no idea we are even regarding him, let alone involving him, somehow, in this sordid conversation. I won't bring up his wife's nether regions.

"Alright, he gets the clock system."

"Well yeah."

Jason Lee leans in, helpful. "See, it's simple. Imagine she's spread eagle on the bed. Looking down, clit is at 12 O'clock, above the lips, below the pubes.

So first, that's how you find it. Second, your first mistake was assuming there's some universal shortcut to orgasm. Every woman's different, dude, and you gotta respect that." Before I can object, he assures me that he never for an instant thought me some insensitive lout. "But I think you do, because Third, if you're attentive and caring enough to find the clitoris in the first place, you'll probably know what to do with it." This is great. I can use this. I mean, it's all sinful, but I can use it. "Fourth, it's not a matter of 'spending too much time on it'. It's just that some guys don't realize that it's very, VERY sensitive, and that direct stimulation can be too much. Be gentle, and not necessarily direct contact. Fifth, fuck Kurt Vonnegut. Pontificating agnostic asshole.' GOD BLESS YOU, MR. DAUTERIVE.

But I sound casual. "Thanks. That's all really helpful, actually."

Jason Lee nods. Nothing to it. But then he wonders, "Hey wait a minute...What do you mean you 'always' thought? I mean, you didn't always know about sex education, right?"

I tried to trace the origins of my hang-up. "Good point. I guess I found out about that particular part of the sexual anatomy some time after 8th grade. And I didn't read *Breakfast of Champions* till college. So I had several years to formulate these ideas." I laugh nervously. The audacity of this conversation! "I can't believe I told you all that. I don't even know you!"

Jason Lee is enthusiastic. He understands perfectly. "That's WHY you can tell me all that. The anonymity of confessing to a stranger often lets us open up to a startling degree. I'm like a doctor. Or a priest. I can't judge you because I don't know you. I'm just a man from the road. We have our brief time together, then we'll part ways, wish each other the best, and our stories remain with each other. And I like to think we've traded a little bit of wisdom in that time."

"Oh. That's really cool." And it is. It's true. He makes it alright, alright.

"So what else is on your mind, sailor?"

I smirk, remembering one of Holden's favorite poems. "Home is the sailor, home from the sea."

"Huh?"

"I spend a lot of time in the past these days." As if that explains everything.

"Is it nice?" He's earnest.

"It goes back and forth." And that's the honest truth.

I remember riding the hayride with Winona at Cox Farms.

"There's the good."

I bite my lip.

I watch Winona walk away at Dulles Airport.

"And the not so good."

Jason Lee nods. "Well you know what they say." He piles some more syrup on his waffles. "The sweet doesn't taste as sweet..."

He fishes the lemon out of his water. Takes a bite of it.

PROFESSOR WILKINSON

Without the sour.

It is night. I am walking out of Fenwick Library. I am alone. My hands are in my pockets and I am downcast. My arms chill in the cool night air. Studying has lost its allure, its intrigue.

I stop. I sigh. What's next? It is a question at least as much philosophical as practical, as eternal as it is immediate. Tonight, do I go to the snack bar or retreat to my room? This life, do I continue to mope over Winona or attempt to move on, whatever that means?

"Ben! Benjamin!"

I am startled. I look to my left.

"Professor?"

I walk to the bushes. Professor Wilkinson is crouched down, looking harried, sleepless, unkempt, and very wild. It has only been several days since I saw him last, but they have been troubled for a number of reasons, and his unsettling appearance now does not help.

"Benjamin. You're alone. Ideal."

I have never seen him like this. It is frightening. "Professor, what's wrong?"

He steps out from the bushes, but he still looks paranoid.

"Where have you been?!" I ask, frantic. I am surprised by the volume and tone of my own voice. The inquiry should have been polite, but he is so manic in approach that he invites a like response.

"My physical whereabouts in recent days are of no matter." He says it as if there were no worry, nothing at all.

I follow him, very concerned. "Yeah, but you haven't been answering your phone, or your e-mail. Everyone's been really concerned."

"Doubtless they had their reasons," which he was clearly brushing off. "Were you followed?"

"What? No." What an odd thing to ask.

I follow Wilkinson as he marches up to the faculty building.

"I suppose I should offer some obligatory mea culpa for neglecting my professional duties."

"You missed three classes." There is, I sense already, something more pressing with higher stakes than that, but it's a starting point.

"But in all honesty, that stagnant world of academia is no longer relevant to you or I. We are on the cusp of a reality beyond the dreams of anything written in those textbooks."

I try to process this. I can't, so instead I point to more practical matters, like the door. "It's locked, Professor. It's after 10 o'clock."

"You think a super-being like myself would be unable to sway security?" The super-being smiles as he holds up his keycard and gains us entry.

I follow him in. He is manically describing unsettling nonsense.

"I had previously indicated that I had reached the limits of what conventional human knowledge could teach us. And knowledge being power, I had naturally climbed to my own personal apex. Or so I thought."

I am exhausted. This was the last thing I needed. I tell him, "I don't need this right now."

The last thing, really. My heart is broken. I hardly need my mind challenged or my sense of fear awoken by whatever fresh Hell this is.

We reach his office.

"I therefore transmuted from conventional Western wisdom and modern scientific viewpoints in favor of Eastern Philosophy and worldwide arcane."

"Winona left."

He doesn't care. "Inconsequential. I am standing on the edge of a great and fathomless precipice, and I want you to bear witness."

His office is an ornate room filled with ancient tomes. We enter and he turns on the lights.

Wilkinson flips through some books. He is possessed by a maniac obsession as chilling as it is frustrating to the observer. "I've sought to unlock some great forgotten knowledge..."

He puts the book down. For once he says nothing. Lets that stand, deep in thought, as the air grows thick and ominous. I want out of this room. A day earlier I may have thought a distraction was ideal. Something to busy me away from all these bothersome emotions. This is not it. This is its own trouble, thoroughly unwelcome and a whole different type of disturbing.

Finally, I break the silence. "What are we doing here?"

He turns to me and smiles benignly. Now I remember the man I admire. He could be intense, sure, and when he got on an academic obsession, there was no deterring him. But it came from a good place, a healthy intellectual pursuit that could be puzzling at times, but ultimately reveals itself as part of a rich and constantly curious character.

He puts his hands on my shoulders in an avuncular manner. This will be his last comforting action. "Benjamin. My boy. Do you know where we are right now?"

"Your office."

"We are about to cross the existential finality." Without a trace of irony or explanation. That smile I found even mildly comforting was a lie. No crack in the manic veneer. I am shaken. I've had enough. If ever I had any control or influence over this situation, and I know I do not, it is time to exercise it.

"Professor, you're really freaking me out."

He crosses to his desk and opens a drawer.

"You will fall down and weep, and understand it all."

● ● ●

It's not like it is, in the movies or at the rifle range with Dad. When there is a loaded gun in a room where there shouldn't be, when it's being held by someone who could do anything...everything you think you know goes out the window. Every sound, however small, shatters a terrible grave-like silence. You're numb, but you're cognizant of every bead of sweat, every itch on your body or crease in your pants, and they're nothing you can do. You've had 400 cups of coffee but you just want to close your eyes and fall into a dreamless black sleep. Time is moving fast as a hurricane, but the world is frozen. You want to scream, but your words come out like whispers in molasses. You can't move. You can breathe. He owns these awful moments. If the trigger is God, then it's an unknowable, implacable deity. Anything you do could set it off. So could doing nothing. You're helpless, hopeless, and utterly, utterly alone.

I try to breathe. "Wait..." is all I can get out, a useless and futile gesture. He won't wait He's ready for this.

"Do you not realize that even now as I speak to you, I am ascending to a higher plane of existence? That nothing you say or think you can do in this reality can sever the fact that I am in this instant reaching the totality of my immortal potential and becoming no less than the godhead of a dimension far beyond ANY of your mere human senses?" His words are absolute. His madness has the immutable finality of prophets and madmen. There's nothing I can do. There's no stopping this now. Maybe there never was. "You can kill this body, but know that I am, as I have always been, and always shall be, a being intrinsically transcending all physical boundaries and philosophical limitations known to man!"

He puts the gun to his head.

WILSON

It doesn't sound anything like it, not really. But it's close enough. Some days, I can't hear a balloon or a door slam without being reminded. So when something pops inside my engine, I'm startled.

I pull to the side of the road. I am in the middle of Kansas.

Some time later, I am still leaning against my car. Aimless. Big blue open sky country. Nothing but fields and fields, and miles and miles, and acre upon acre of corn, corn, corn. The purity of that, the simplicity, the necessity.

And those clouds again. Those same clouds. It is both comforting and terrifying to find them above me again. What a sky. So easy, I think, to be swallowed up completely, to be enveloped by one of those masses of white dreams, to be carried away until we dissipate in the sun. How simple it must be, to surrender to the float.

I'm in no rush. I could call AAA, but I take these moments when they come.

In the distance, a truck pulls up.

Ed Wilson is 72 or thereabouts, a genial, well-traveled Good Old Boy, of a different sort than Jason Lee. He takes a look at my popped hood.

"Son, you picked a heck of a place to break down."

"Bad?"

"I seen worse. But I can't fix ya. Can't tow ya either. Not with my current rig. But I can be a good Christian, give you a ride into town. They should fix you up there. Send somebody to pick her up."

He starts to walk to his truck. I look at my car.

"Is it safe to just leave it here?"

He spreads his arms, indicating the broad emptiness. "Way out here?"

For once, the emptiness is comforting.

Wilson has a dashboard Jesus and a cross hanging from the mirror. On the back window is a sticker saying "Not all who wander are lost". Several times I think about asking what he's hauling, but I decide it's not interesting. Probably corn. Why fill the cabin with banal small talk? I owe him more than that.

"Town's not too much further," he informs me. Then, after a moment, he says with significance, "It's Holcomb, by the way."

That stirs something, but I can't place it. "Holcomb. Sounds familiar."

"Yeah. I expect as it should. Couple of grisly murders out there, way back. Shocked the nation."

"Wait. You mean...*In Cold Blood*?"

"The very same. You know, we're not actually too far from the old Clutter place."

"Aw, geez. I read that book."

"Book? Heck, I remember when it happened!" he clucks forlornly. "Only a pup myself at the time, but I remember. Gave me some nightmares."

I look out the window at the passing Kansas countryside. It looks so calm and peaceful. Yet there is no secure place. The world is out there, no matter where you go. Not all who wander are lost, but wherever they wander to, can they ever truly be safe?

Wilson goes on. "Those boys, they got it in their heads there was thousands in that house. Weren't no such thing. Just a brutal, senseless sin."

I remember. "Right. They only found like less than 50 bucks in the house."

Wilson shook his head, agreeing with the facts but commenting on the takeaway. "And that's the coda. That's the end of the chapter and we're supposed to cluck our tongues and say 'Four people killed for less than 50 dollars'." Doesn't make sense to him. "Well the way the reporters always presented that fact never quite sat right with me, I have to say. As if an insufficient return is the real horror of it. Because what would make it worth it? If they had found the ten grand they were expecting, would that make shooting a 16-year-old girl in the face worth it?"

Grim. "I guess not."

"Bless my soul, not. And maybe that's the worst of it. Because it was about the money. They weren't killers by trade, Hickock and Smith weren't no Leopold and Loeb. But they had it in them. They justified it somehow. Get rid of the witnesses. And maybe that makes sense on a practical level, but that's the only way it does make sense. I just can't imagine what that does to your soul. Look a 16 year old girl in the eye, a 15-year-old boy, shoot them in the head."

I wince. Inwardly, I hear the bang of Wilkinson shooting himself in the head. Very different motives, Leopold, Loeb, Hickock, Smith, and Wilkinson, but the end result was always the same.

Wilson notices my discomfort. "I don't mean to bring you down, son."

Nor I him. But there are some things that stay with you, and you can't talk about in polite society. Things so bad you screw up just trying to explain why you can't talk about it.

"No, it just...I've seen someone...shot in the head. I mean, if it's murder, or if it's self-defense, or...or they do it to themselves. It just...It looks bad. You don't...You don't forget that."

I stand solemnly at Wilkinson's funeral, a stale, desultory affair. I am still in shock, still processing what cannot be processed or unseen. Holden pats me consolingly on the shoulder, but I shake it off.

I sit in Professor Skarsgård's Germanic Mythology Class. My mind is elsewhere and elsewhen.

His words are muted, indistinct. He is talking about how Tolkien, like Wagner, was very much operating in the Germanic epic tradition. On another day, I would have been very interested in this subject.

I get up. I can't take much more of this.

Skarsgård watches me walk out. He is a compassionate man. He empathizes with me. Right now, I won't take his wisdom or his kindness.

I pack up my dorm room, leaving it behind as bare and empty as I feel.

I arrive at LAX Airport. Dad is there to greet me with a hug that can't be as comforting as it needs to be.

•   •   •   •   •

I walk along Santa Monica Beach. I'm a continent away from where it happened. But it's still so close. The ebb and flow of the tide, always receding as it always returns, is precious little comfort. Still, I like to listen. I like to close my eyes and listen to that tidal gravity, that unbroken continuity of water and sand. I can pretend, for a moment, that some things last forever, as it washes in and out, again and again, without paying mind to the weight on my heart or the burden on my soul. All the Earth knows of eternal return.

I get settled in a job at Carter and Stone. Nobody resents the nepotism. The pay is decent and I excel, on a technical level. I go to work. Dull to it.

•   •   •   •   •

I eat lunch in the break room alone. I am polite with my co-workers but remain detached. A few details, I am acutely aware, have reached their ears. They withhold their pity, if they feel any, but I can feel it in the air, and it makes me cringe.

Adjusting to the LA lifestyle, I take yoga. It feels affected. But still relaxing. It's a strain. I stretch my body out of proportion. I get worn out.

Nina, my instructor, says pleasant things, affirmations of the spirit of yoga. Some stick with me.

"May all beings be happy and peaceful."

My co-worker Mike tries casual conversation. He has a fondness for Fantasy Football and something called The Dropkick Murphys. He tells me he is having a party tonight. He is inviting me out of pity. I would have preferred it if the invitation came out of a desire to get in my father's good graces.

The party rages on at Mike's house. It has become a dull roar to me as I stand in the corner alone, red cup in hand, solemn, somber if not sober, as I ignore the festivity around me. I have paid my obligatory small talk. Now, I linger. I don't know what I am doing here. I drink more. The women are beautiful, but I can think of nothing to say. I shouldn't have come.

• • • • •

Dave and Jim see me from across the room. I can imagine their conversation.

"Hey, isn't that Carter's son?"

"Yeah it is."

"I thought the boss man said he was going to some big school back east."

"George Mason, in Virginia."

"Yeah, right. Didn't his professor try to kill him or something?"

"Nah, he got out okay. Professor killed himself."

"Damn. What happened then?"

"He dropped out."

"Why?"

"I guess he couldn't cope."

And they'd be right.

I drift through this party, pretending to have a good time. KV said we are what we pretend to be, but maybe that's one more thing he was wrong about, because it doesn't appear to be working. I want to pretend to be happy. I want to pretend to be normal. I want to pretend that nothing I've been worrying about matters very much, and that this is just a party.

"Do you think Danny Elfman is anti-Semitic?"

There is at least one interesting guy there. That's not fair. There are no supporting characters in life. Everyone's the lead in their own story, and, I'm sure, interesting in their own right.

I should clarify, then, one guy who engages my interests this particular night, at this very party. His name is Trent Malloy. He was a "semi-struggling" screenwriter who was moonlighting as a private investigator while negotiating the deal for his pilot. Said pilot was called "Mermaid Squad", and with that title I don't really need to describe it.

We play beer pong, neither very invested in the outcome. He drinks "Snake Bite", which is half lager (in this case the hipster elixir Pabst Blue

Ribbon) and cider (Wyder's Pear, which he brought himself). He tells me that his ex-girlfriend got him interested in this particular libation. He makes several vague references to her throughout the night. I sense he thinks there must have been a compelling story there, but I don't bother to ask. All his allusions stir in me is the realization that other people might not find Winona and my love story interesting. I suppose it goes to what I said about us all being the lead in our own lives. I'm recounting what happened between me and the woman I love(d?). Whether anyone else would care to read is secondary. There's something cathartic in simply the release, putting these words down and letting them sit, tangibly in the universe.

And I have no idea what to make of his question, which comes completely out of left field.

"Do you think Danny Elfman is anti-Semitic?"

"You know, I never really thought about it." I'm drunk enough by this point that I can accept with simplicity all that comes to me. And I'm still so sober that I don't laugh at the absurdity of the query.

Trent figures. "Neither had I. It had never occurred to me. Then one day I got thinking about Danny Elfman. I've always loved him as a composer. You know, *Batman, Hulk, Spider-Man...*"

"*Nightmare on Elm Street.*" One of Winona's favorites.

"Right, and Darkman–"

"I meant the *Nightmare Before Christmas*," I correct. Freddy Kruger had never come up between us.

"Sure. And *Edward Scissorhands* and *The Flash*. The list goes on and on," he started drunkenly sing-songing, "*and on my friend.*" He chuckles. "Everybody loves him. I guess my ex-girlfriend– she was a singer– maybe she was influenced..." But he digresses, realizing that this was too tenuous "Anyway, I got interested in his career before Burton. Because I had heard about his band. The Mystic Knights of the Oingo-Boingo. They made a movie, back in 1980. *The Forbidden Zone.* I had heard of it, didn't really know what it was about. You seen it?"

"No."

"Neither had I. I looked it up on Wikipedia, and I saw that it had been criticized for being anti-Semitic. And that just threw me off! It was so bizarre. How could Danny Elfman, of all people, be an anti-Semite? It just didn't click."

"So is he? Or was he? I mean-""Right. So I Netflixed *The Forbidden Zone*, to see what all the fuss was about. It turns out there's one character who's a bit of a Jewish stereotype. Borscht Belt, 'Oy Vey' type. And that's it. He's a good guy, not portrayed in a sinister way or anything. He just has an accent. And that's it."

"Huh."

"I mean, it doesn't get any more stereotypical or offensive than, I don't know, Billy Crystal in *The Princess Bride*, or an Adam Sandler supporting character, or the granddad in *Hey Arnold*. And it turns out that Danny Elfman is Jewish himself! So the whole thing is pointless!"

As is this conversation? "Ok?" I really don't see where he's going, or if he's already arrived.

He can appreciate my confusion, he just begs me to indulge him, because he is going somewhere, like it or not.

"Look, the point isn't whether Danny Elfman is anti-Semitic or not- he's not, that we've established- but that's not the point. I mean it is, but..." He takes a breath. Gathers his thoughts. "Okay, my point is this: Why did I find it so absurd a concept that Danny Elfman could possibly be anti-Semitic?"

"I don't know." I have to admit, a good question, so long as we were on the subject (which was not a good topic).

"Right I don't know! I didn't! What did I know about Danny Elfman? I knew what his music sounded like, all that 'La-la-la-la-la-la-la, boom-boom-boom-boom, didi-didi-didly-dee!' I knew what he looked like. I knew who he worked with. But that was it. He could have harbored some horrible prejudice, for all I knew. So why not?"

"Well, uh, he works in Hollywood?"

Admittedly, that wasn't a very PC thing of me to say. But it's true, isn't it? There are a lot of Jewish people in Hollywood, which is a very liberal place. How could a raging anti-Semite, even one as musically talented as Elfman, become such a legend there if there was any legitimacy to these claims of bigotry?

"Tell that to Mel Gibson and Marlon Brando. It's possible, my friend, it's possible. So what then? His sensibilities? Nah. It's Gothic, dark, orchestral. Wagner was anti-Semitic. There are no words to convey an outrage at Deicide or deny the Holocaust, nothing to describe his feelings towards Israel's right to exist one way or the other. And you think just because he does Tim Burton movies- what, a bunch of dark spires and living corpses, that means he can't hate on Judaism?"

I feel strangely compelled to defend what didn't need to be defended. I suppose we all had that innate sense we walked around with, something we didn't even realize until it was presented to us, that Danny Elfman, whatever else he may be, was no anti-Semite.

"You um, I don't know, look at his fans?" Like Winona, of Jewish extraction and a huge admirer herself.

"What about them?" Trent prods, as if he's considered this himself.

"You know…" What did I mean? "I guess you go to Hot Topic, and the kids there are pretty liberal and stuff?"

It was weak, and he attacks my weakness with glee.

"Exactly! So what! A bunch of suburban white Goths like a certain kind of music, and that means the guy who composed it must be bigotry free?"

"I also get the sense that a lot of them are bisexual?"

He nods. "Sure. So these girls, these white suburban girls, they watch and sing along to *Nightmare Before Christmas*, then go to a graveyard to drink wine and make out, and the conclusion is…what, exactly?"

I sigh. "I give up. You're right. I guess Danny Elfman could have been anti-Semitic for all I knew. I'm glad he's not though."

Trent nods, agreeing enthusiastically with both statements. "I guess you never really know people."

Later in the night. Trent leaves sometime before midnight. The party rages on. Should I have left by now? I don't care. I sit blankly on the couch. I am drunk, but not drunk enough. I was talking to Danielle earlier, a friend of Mike's but not a girlfriend, he emphasized before introducing us. Danielle, a cute blonde software developer with a sympathetic ear. I probably had more than a fair "shot" at her, to use the gutter mentality of a drunken hook-up culture, a world I was simultaneously enchanted and repelled by. But that isn't me. Or so I tell myself. After Winona, I really don't know.

The music, alcohol, drugs, and sex surrounding me fade into the background and become a blur of light and sound as I sink deeper into my numbness.

I sit next to Wilson in his big rig, having just given him a sense of my troubled state of mind.

"Well," The old man starts compassionately. He doesn't pretend to understand, which I like, but he has heart. "That's a bad break, son. Ain't no sense in it. And sometimes it looks like there ain't no sense anywhere. But you gotta believe God has a plan, that his roadmap is open, and Jesus is gonna show you that path."

I nod. I don't disagree. But it's so hard. "I just don't get it."

"Well you seen my truck, right?"

"Sure"

"Had to put a sticker on my rig, 'OVERSIZE LOAD', as if my truck is too big for the road. But see, I don't believe that's it. Cause if we lived in a world without laws, with no highway signs or traffic cops, who's to say what's too big for anything?" His point is simple, but earnest, and I can tell it doesn't just apply to trucking. "You look up and down this world, I don't believe you'll find the answer. I been from Missoula to St. Augustine, and I never seen a man too big for this world, and this world only being one of many. And by this point, I reckon the load's not too big, it's the mind's too small. That's a funny thing too, because they say the brain has an infinite capacity for thought which does not diminish for the experience. A road with too many trucks on it fills up. But a mind with too many ideas just grows, I suppose. But don't ask me. I just know my rig. You can slap a sticker on a truck, get one with less axles, do what you will. That all's easy. Wrapping your head around a new idea, that's what's hard." He chuckles. "Anyway, that's just a roundabout way of saying, none of us can really see the big picture. Not all of it anyway. We just have to keep on keeping on and trust The Lord to keep our back."

I hear what he is saying. And I dig it. Such a kind old man, wise in a simple, folksy way. He reminds me of my Grandfather. And what he is saying rings true in my ears. Trust The Lord to keep my back.

I am just trying to find The Lord in all this, trying to see just where my back is going, and what will become of me as a result.

Wilson pulls up to the old auto garage. Gus, the man in stained green overalls, stands outside, working on a car. He looks up when he sees the truck pull, Wilson stops. I open the door.

"Go with God, Ben. If you're looking, he'll show you the way." He smiles warmly, like a grandfather.

"Thank you." It's all I can say, but it's enough.

And then he drives off, a Good Samaritan with road-tested wisdom and a friendly ear, another Christian I've been blessed to know.

•　　•　　•　　•　　•

Gus takes a look at my engine as I watch.

"Durndest thing," he says, poking fun at his own speech. "Dorn"dest.

"So..."

"I gotcha."

Gus works on the hood. It's a sea of troubles under there. I've never been terribly mechanically inclined myself, and now that I find myself in a tight spot, I'm grateful for the help of a real expert, even if it exposes my inadequacy in this field.

Luckily, I'm not even more insecure than I really am, or I might find myself questioning my manhood. That's superficial though, and not really of concern. Cars are not my thing. So what? Move on. Gus knows what he's doing, and I'm paying him, and the problem will be solved, and then I will move on, literally. It doesn't matter if he is quietly judging me all the while for failing to deal on my own terms with my own abilities (or lack thereof) what may be for him, and other red-blooded American males, a routine problem easily enough solved by anybody who isn't a complete pantywaist.

Not that Gus is necessarily thinking any of that, of course. I'm projecting, once again. We all do it. Even Gus, I think. He's got to be making assumptions about his customers one way or another. Do we frustrate him with our petty problems, or does he like us, grateful for the business? It's a shame I don't have more time to get to know him, that our relationship must be so mercenary, because he really is helping me out. God forbid I be stranded here, in-

In the middle of nowhere. Is what I was thinking, but it's such a trite cliché, so unkind, so unfair. So inaccurate. There are no supporting characters in real life, and everywhere is somewhere to somebody. Back East was now my somewhere, and perhaps there would be someone waiting at that somewhere for me. I didn't know.

But this place, this small desert town with its few trees and simple gas station, was somewhere, it was Gus's somewhere.

After a while, I break the silence. I realize that my recounting of this story, philosophical as its nature may be, reaches the point of straining credulity. Does everyone really talk like that? Have you met a single soul who didn't feel the need to wax poetic and pontificate about the meaning of life?

So I force a deconstruction. "Aren't you going to say something profound?"

"Say again?"

"Are you gonna offer me advice, or some perspective on life?"

Gus looks at me funny. "Now why would I do that?"

"Everybody else seems to."

Gus distinguishes himself by not saying anything particularly special. "I'm no fancy boy. I just fix your car." Gus takes off his shirt, sweating under the hard work. "Gotta stick to your skill set," he says simply.

WEIGHTS

"I can do anything!" Holden declares his own superiority, dead lifting a ludicrous amount of weight, admiring himself in the mirror. Scooter, a long-haired stoner type and unlikely friend to Holden watches, impressed.

He raised the bar above his head triumphantly. "Because I am invincible!"

His acolyte applauds. "Yeah you are. Yeah, you are man!"

I sit at one of the weight machines, only working out lethargically.

"Whatever you say, Holden."

Holden grunts as he sets the weight down. He put the weight down, but he picked up my tone.

"And what can you do, Ben?"

Holden shakes off Scooter's handing him another weight and approaches me. I brace myself for the lecture I know is coming.

"I don't know," I answer lamely. "Major in Philosophy? Write a thesis with no real-world application?"

He knows what's really getting me down, so he tries to follow my distraction. "And how is the Professor?"

"Sick, I guess. He didn't show up to class yesterday."

Holden strolls over, standing directly over me. He is such an imposing figure, and even a casual inquiry seems like a demand. "You seem distraught, soldier. I suppose little miss so-and-so is still haunting you with her recent departure."

I feel obligated to defend her honor or my pride, but it all comes out weak. "Hey, don't call her that...whatever that means."

Holden helps himself to the heaviest hand weights. This conversation was inevitable.

"Truth be told, I really liked Winona. I never told her that." A rare moment of introspection. "We were fundamentally opposed on most arenas of human thought, yet I admired her tenacity and attitude. She smoked with little regard to society's disapproval and she provided ample intellectual challenge." He smirks provocatively. "I could see myself having to 'conquer' a woman like that."

"Hey, lay off!"

Scooter is watching the gym's TV as he lazily tries a very light dumbbell. An M&M commercial plays.

"That brown M&M is such a bitch."

I know what she means. Ms. Brown still feels relatively new, but like Scooter, I have yet to adjust to her or her self-satisfied, dismissive attitude. I suppose after the over-sexualized Green M&M, the Mars corporation wanted to introduce a positive female role model. So they came up with an intellectual chocolate woman (hence the glasses), but her entire schtick seems to be aggressive aggravation that people think her brown shell is no shell, that she's walking around naked. I guess I never really thought about their colored shells being clothes, but her commercials focus solely on that conceit.

It's an honest mistake, but she takes it too far. One thread is her quietly simmering anger at the Red M&M for getting it wrong. Fine, maybe she should get a thicker skin, but whatever. But then she sets him up to be devoured? Insanity.

"Hush, Scooter," Holden admonishes, then turns to me. "I'm extolling her virtues for your benefit. Her feminine influence has a positive effect on your disposition." That's Holden all over. He would sound pretentious if he didn't have the presentation to back up his manner. "I liked seeing you have a girlfriend."

"And I still do."

He is not convinced. "Do you suppose she's getting hogged by a filthy Frenchman in her Parisian dormitory even now as we speak?"

"Jeepers, Holden!"

"Consider." His tone is smooth, as always. Nothing rattles him as he rattles others. Sometimes I don't know why we're friends.

"No. No! First of all, her program's in Vienna, not Paris. She switched. I told you that."

"An Austrian then. Your fraulein may be getting stuffed by our next governator."

"Absolutely not. We're still together." I add, "You Neanderthal" to emphasize that he was the wrong one.

"Together, with the Atlantic between you."

His questions grate me, perhaps because they articulate, albeit crudely, concerns I have been having myself. "Yes. Long distance."

"And how has your correspondence been?"

Cuts to the core.

"She's...been busy. Settling in."

"Interesting."

I stop lifting weights. He needs to be corrected. He's never admitted fault or changed his mind in his life, but I must make an attempt. "Holden, I like to think my *Philia* for you is unconditional, but you're pushing it right now!"

"Philia?"

"It's one of The Four Loves. Friendship"

"Then I'll be a friend. And real friends don't lie to each other for hollow comfort. Look at me, Ben. Mankind's inability to front reality and accept the truth for what it is, is the source of so much of his woe. Eve knew the serpent for what he was. We would be spared all this if she was honest with herself."

There is no malice in his speech or his motivation. What hurts most of all, there may be honesty there.

"Shut the fuck up. It's a separation, not a break-up."

He nods, patronizing. "Ah. Euphemisms. Word-Play Wordplay. Doublespeak. The favorite deception of public and self alike. War becomes 'a police action'. Infanticide becomes 'women's reproductive rights'. Socialism is 'social reform', and we have always been at war with Eastasia."

I don't respond. He's meandering, so I act like I don't see the points. Instead, I start to lift the weights with a fury.

"Or how about 'Islam is a religion of peace'" Have you read The Koran?"

I shake my head between lifts. Good. Let him digress. We all know how smart you are, Holden. Give us a lecture.

"Way back, I wanted to understand who I was trying to kill, and who was trying to kill me. So I read The Koran. And I read as many Hadith as I could get my hands on. Their prophetic traditions. And there's a lot of interesting stuff there, young Benjamin. It's really worth a look. But somewhere along my research I come across a debate. And that argument is whether Muhammad, The Prophet. Whether he..." Holden attempted darkly amused detachment, but I could detect a palpable disgust. "...actually penetrated his six-year-old wife, or simply rubbed his member on her thighs until he finished. And it was then I realized I was dealing with true depravity. Real evil. We're not talking about something that was perverted, for you can only corrupt something that was good and pure in the first place. We're talking about something that always was, and always will be perverse." I stop for a second, his opportunity to say, "You have to call things as they are."

I just lift more. Holden encourages this.

"Yes. Yes! Get angry!"

I adjust the weights. Put more on. I keep lifting. I want to drown it all out. Holden, Winona, everything.

"More. More, boy! Channel that!"

I strain. It just doesn't stop.

"Soar! No woman can hold you!"

I put the weights down with a collapsing sigh. I want to scream. "So what's your point?!"

Holden takes on a quieter, more compassionate tone.

"Truth, Ben. You have to stop lying to yourself. Winona left."

"And she's not coming back."

•   •   •

Holden's words stay with me as I drive through Iowa alone.

I stop the car. Pull to the side of the road. Open the glove compartment.

Winona's letter. A Rubik's Cube. Two things I've never really solved.

An old bar napkin. It's a drawing. One of hers, of course. Me as a werewolf, embracing her as a witch.

I smile, remembering.

I stand outside Danny's Bar, looking up at the stars.

I am surprised by Winona, who runs into my side with a hug.

"Hello!" I say, pleasantly startled.

She kisses me. "Read your story, wolf boy!"

I am pleased, but nervous. "Oh yeah?" I venture.

"Bout halfway through. BUT I have gotten to the most interesting part. So far."

"So far."

"Den of the Wolf Queen," she grins, giving it the appropriate allure and mystery.

●　　　●　　　●　　　●　　　●

A frosty, treacherous peak. Four big, hairy men, warrior types, kick along their prisoner up the mountain. Sven, Fury, Talos and Spike are fierce, lumbering and bloodthirsty. Trip, about 20 or so, bare chest in this frigid air. Wearing only a ragged pair of jeans and a wooden cross. Barefoot in the snow, it hits his feet like knives. His hair is untamed. His eyes are deep and blue and contain an innocence untarnished by the horror he's been through.

Trip McConnell had been captured by The Blood Pack. He had vowed to never come in their grasp again.

"I don't know why we don't just bite him up now," Fury growls. "Seems like a waste of good meat."

Talos grabs one of Trip's arms. "If you call this good meat."

"Oh, just let me," Spike whines. "Let me! Let me!"

"Close your jaws, pups." Sven's voice is gruff and absolute. "She'll do with him what she will." He shoves Trip. "Maybe then she'll throw us a bone."

Trip looks up to the cave ahead, a fire glowing from inside. He feared the monsters around him, because he knew he was once one of them, and his greatest nightmare...was that they would take him again.

The entrance to the cave is veiled with leather patches, the floor covered in fur and blankets. A fire burns in the center. A large room, mostly dark, with a circle of light in the center. Just outside of the circle of light is a throne where a hooded figure sits in the darkness. The silhouette is visible in the shadows, but indistinct. The men shove Trip in, on his knees. Trip tries to rise, but Sven kicks him in the back. Trip gathers his breath.

"Kneel," Sven seethes.

Trip remains on his knees. He tries to catch his breath in this frigid air and listens to the ominous silence. He tries to pierce the darkness with his eyes, but the figure doesn't move.

Finally.

Her voice comes out of the darkness. Rita steps into the light, and they see her at last. She is an attractive, dark-haired woman, perhaps in her 30s. She wears a strange, green, almost medieval robe with a Robin Hood like hood, and a fur coat around her shoulders. Rita takes the hood off.

She smiles warmly at Trip.

"The prodigal son returns."

Trip looks away. "I'm no kin of yours."

"Aren't you?" She turns to her men. "Leave us."

Sven protests, "But Lady Rita-"

"-LEAVE!" Her voice takes on a ferocious quality, and the men scamper out obediently.

Rita smiles warmly at Trip. "My boys are rough. You must keep a short leash. Must discipline."

Trip avoids her gaze. Rita kneels down to his level.

She studies him. Gazes at his body. She smells him, a move he winces from.

"Do you remember when we first met, Trip?" she chuckles. "High school."

A couple years earlier, yet a lifetime ago. A guidance counselor's office in a quiet east Texas suburb. Rita opens the door and enters. Trip stands up. He has no idea what's ahead. Rita sits down at her desk and smiles warmly. For all her powers, neither does she.

He has been bitten, not by her. A stray wolf escaped from her pack. Already Trip is beginning to feel the changes, and it frightens him. He hopes this adult will tell him something about rage, about change. Real human lessons he can apply to his supernatural secret, something he cannot share with her.

For her part, Rita thinks this is just puberty. She took this job on a lark, something to sate her boredom until the next Blood Harvest. But she does care about the children. She allows that. She will guide with her counsel.

And in Trip, already, she senses something. She offers him friendship, she offers him counsel. He feels both, and something more than that. Something primal, something pubescent, something preternatural and all those things.

She can sense he is drawn to her in more ways than one, and she likes it.

"I'm here to help you."

* * * * *

Trip shakes his head at the memory.

"Another one of your lies."

She has no regrets. "When you live as long as I do, you have to take on many faces." She kneels down before Trip. She cradles his cross between her fingers. "We have no problem with this." She kisses the cross. "We are not vampires."

"I'm not."

Rita breaks away from Trip and walks into the circle. "We. We, we, we, Trip. You must think of it that way again. And what are we?"

"That was the worst month of my life," Trip answers bitterly. "I'm never going back."

"No, you loved it." Rita gently insists. "Part of you still thirsts for your snapping maw at the moon."

Trip steadies his breathing. This is difficult. "I was so close to shedding innocent blood. I could have done..." he clenches. "Horrible things."

Rita is at his side. "Also great things." She comes closer. "You have been latent recently. You 'cured' yourself." She states with a mixture of amusement and disdain. 'But the wound still runs deep, and the power is in your blood." She looks at Trip's upper left arm, the scar of his bite. "This is where

Stephen..." She traces her fingers along the wound gently. Trip winces but does not step back from her touch. "It hurt so much, didn't it?"

"'He made me into an animal."

"He was...a disappointment." Rita concedes, "And now he's gone. It should have been me. I would have been gentle." She continues to run her fingers over Trip's skin. "But you..." Giving him goosebumps. "You're different, aren't you?"

"I'm g-good." Trip's voice shakes.

Rita ignores the moral judgment. Makes her own declarations. "I am savage and I am terrible and I am great and I am beautiful and I am mighty." He can't disagree. "Not man. Not beast. Nor something in between. We are more. Lords and ladies of the Earth. And we are of the Earth, for we are wild, and the wild is ours. It's wonderful, being a beast, isn't it?"

She howls, a loud, rollicking echo rich with boldness and beauty.

"Such power. Don't you love it?" she leans in to Trip. Puts her ear to his mouth. "Do you still howl?" She looks him in the eyes. "Will you let me hear?"

"I will never come back." Trip is defiant. Shaking, but defiant.

Rita stands up. "Have I not been good to you, Trip? Have I not been a good mother?"

This outrages him. "You're not-"

"I made you," she answers simply. "I turned the one who turned you. What you are, what you can be, that is because I choose you. I gave you that strength. I gave you that will." She touches the side of Trip's face, compassionate. "You're a wolf." Trip looks up. "Be proud of it."

Rita sits in her throne. She pats her lap.

"Come, my cub. Come into my lap and be clove to me."

Trip rises.

●　　●　　●　　●　　●

"But then the chapter ends!" Winona is excited.

"There's more on the way," I assure her.

"I hope so, cause I'm in suspense...and that's not a bad thing." She playfully punches me. "So come on! Does he become a werewolf or what? Do Trip and Lady Rita do it?"

"'Do it'?" I question her phrase.

"Oh come on! Don't tell me the obvious erotic underpinnings were not intentional!"

"No, of course it's there. This is horror laced with the erotic, like Clive Barker. It's just not going to get hard-core, like bad Twilight fan fiction."

"That line, 'Be clove to me.' What's that about?"

"Oh. Antiquated past tense of 'cleave', which can mean be close to, join. Genesis 2:24, 'Therefore shall a man leave his father and his mother and shall cleave unto his wife: and they shall be one flesh.'"

"Hmm," Winona ponders.

"Yeah, it's all implicitly sexual. Like if she said 'Be clove' kind of fast, that could sound like 'Make love'".

"Or more explicit." Winona raises her eyes. "You know what the other definition of cleave is, right? Is he gonna split her in half?"

"Gross."

"Like an old piece of firewood." She is enjoying this.

"No, no. Lady Rita is the Queen of the Blood Pack. She would absolutely be dominant."

"Well is that what you're into? Wolves and howling and moons and all that?"

"Hey, it's not a 'Tale of the Inane', but it is a story."

Winona kisses me, then turns my head around, whispering in my ear, her hot breath on my skin. 'On a hot summer night, would you offer your throat to the wolf with the red roses?" She gently bites my neck.

I am thrown for a loop, not in an unpleasant fashion. "Well. I am officially turned on."

She raises her eyebrows, pleased and intrigued. "Yeah? What do you want to do about it?"

I awkwardly try to dodge the question. "We better go inside. Your friends are waiting."

"Kinky."

"So is Holden."

"Kinkier."

I turn to enter the bar. "He's probably doing pinball."

"Jodie Foster?"

We sit around the table with Winona's friends, Ayishah, Agatha, Lori, and Lori's boyfriend Michael. They are intellectual, and they are refined. I feel out of place among them. I worry, secretly but consciously, about being discovered as a fraud, a poser. Surely they will soon discern, perhaps they know it already, that I am not one of them. That I'm not as hip, that I don't have the right opinions. And they may not approve.

And then I think of Chris Isaak again, and of versatility, and how his seamless fusion of soulful country and Roy Orbison-esque pop can be applied to my own situation. How one man can sound as natural in a Tennessee honky tonk as a San Francisco coffee shop. People are complex. Our sensibilities are apt to change, and we make a lot of friends. It's something not to be shunned, but celebrated.

In the background, Holden is indeed pinballing up a storm.

"So, Ben," Aiyshah drolly inquires, "How goes Dead White Male Studies?"

Winona starts to draw something on a bar napkin.

"It's a living," I answer. I don't want to get into that. It's tired and I have no defense. Despite, or perhaps because of the overwhelming opinions of those around me, I eschew taking political stands myself. It's also part of my naturally submissive nature. And she's right. Most the philosophers we read, analyze, praise, and disregard are dead white males. Two out of three on Wilkinson himself.

Holden scores major points. He raises his arms in triumph.

"I am a champion!"

Scooter, standing next to Holden, high-fives him. "Yeah man!"

Aiyshah continues, "And you don't think Wilkinson's tunnel vision focus on an almost exclusively phallocentric view of existentialism contributes to the patriarchal tradition of higher academia?"

"Uh...I hadn't actually thought of that." I really haven't. I don't know what that means. I think Aiyshah's legitimate concerns may be swallowed up in word soup and pretentious diction. Sometimes it's just best to say it straightforward.

Winona slides me the bar napkin. Me as a wolf, her as a witch. I smile.

"Typical." Aiyshah rolls her eyes.

Winona smiles back.

STACEY

I drive through the suburbs of Chicago, the city skyline visible in the distance. Those Dreamland clouds fade and darken, and an ominous feel looms over the city as white turns to gray.

I pull up to Stacey and Nelson's house. Stacey, my older sister, comes running out of the house. She is a Hitchcock blonde still wearing her green hospital scrubs.

"Ben!"

I come out of the car and we hug. "Hey Stacey."

She touches my face. We have been apart for so long. "How are you, Ben?"

We sit on the couch. I attempt to answer her question. It is just a standard banality, most likely, and I'm supposed to say "Fine" and move on. But I yearn for more than that, and Stacey being the accepting person she is, she will indulge me.

"I mean. I guess I'm doing better. Maybe that's time. Maybe it's the continent away. Or the work. It's a good distraction."

She's concerned. "Are you sure that's healthy? Did you give yourself enough time to process it?"

It's a question I've often asked myself. "What is the proper amount of time? I mean, I didn't...I didn't stop it from happening-"

"Stop."

"No. I just..."

She is emphatic. "At the hospital, I see all sorts of damaged people. And it's not just their bodies. People's minds get sick too, Ben. You can't put that on yourself.

I know she's right. "That's what they keep telling me."

"Cause it's true. Now, about the future.

"The future?"

Stacey gets up. "Dinner."

I watch Stacey chop vegetables. Tell her what's on my mind, whether she wants to hear it or not. She did invite this, after all.

"She never called. She never wrote. Didn't send one e-mail. Doesn't that mean she doesn't care?"

"Well she sent you this letter."

"Yeah. First contact in over a year."

"Well obviously you still care or you wouldn't be driving across the country just to see her."

Good point. I don't know what I feel. "Maybe I want closure. It was just so unceremonious. An actual breakup would have been better. That would have been something. If she had shouted or given me a reason. This...not with a bang but with a whimper...It's just numb."

Stacey is aggravated. Maybe I'm wearing her out. Maybe I just have to listen. I have been doing a lot of that lately, and it seems to work, or at the very least grant me some respite from my own troubled thoughts. "God, Ben. They say, oh, 'the opposite of love isn't hate, it's indifference'. As if apathy is worse than anger. Pardon my preference, but I think that's one of those dehumanizing clichés people like to cling to. Because loneliness is like drowning, and if you're falling, you try to take someone with you, and if they don't go down with you, you call them indifferent, as if that's worse. Tragedy plus time is comedy? Who thought of that? I first found out about genocide when I was 9, and I still don't think it's any funnier. Dracula was a real person, you know. He impaled his enemies' heads on stakes and forced them to eat their friends. Now kids dress up like him for Halloween. I'm not a cynic. Really, I'm not. And I don't think I have anything profound to say. Just next time you're drowning, don't look to the person next to you and try to drag them down. Don't ask them why they're not sinking. Ask them how they're still floating. Ask them to help you up. Maybe they will. I can't promise you'll live longer, but you just might live better."

I get that. But I tease her. "What is it with this family and aquatic metaphors?"

She throws a baby carrot at me. "Oh yeah, how is Dad's boat?"

"You mean Stacey?"

"Aww." She still gets a kick out of that. "And how's the captain?"

"He's fine, Stace, just fine. Business is booming, and he's...yeah, very affable."

"Affable?"

"Yeah, it's just a new dynamic. Just me and him."

"Two swinging bachelors?" she winks.

"No, hah, well," I laugh nervously, "he's not exactly Chris Isaak in The Informers."

"Didn't see it."

"I think he is dating though. Through church. You should come out, obviously."

"I'll think about it. Make some time this summer."

"You know you're part of the reason for the road trip too. I could have just flown out to DC in a month, when she gets there. But this way I get to see the country. Gather my thoughts. Visit you and Holden."

"Who's Holden?"

"He's..." I trail off. Something else is on my mind. The elephant in the room. "Have you talked to-" "-Don't," she cuts me off. Gentle but firm. She's right. We don't need to go there.

The house door opens. In walks Nelson, a tall, grim, and humorless man. Also the love of her life.

"Hey babe. Look who's here!"

Nelson sees me and his face falls, not overly pleased to see his brother-in-law. But he quickly recovers and puts on a polite smile.

I stand up. Nelson greets me with a firm handshake.

"Benjamin. I thought you weren't getting in till tonight."

"Well it is after six," Stacey helpfully points out.

"It's good to see you Nelson. It's been a while."

Nelson puts his arm around Stacey. He smiles. This one is sincere. "Likewise."

I look at the happy couple with a twinge of whimsy. Envious smile. Whatever else they are, they're happy. "How long you guys been married now?" I don't get it. I don't get them. But I never got my parents as a couple either. Does anyone?

"Coming up on three years," Nelson answers proudly.

"Wow. The Turquoise Anniversary."

I laugh. I'm the only one. It was a dumb joke, if it could even be called that.

"Food," Stacey helpfully reminds us.

I sit with my brother-in-law and his wife around their dinner table. We have our heads bowed and hold hands as Nelson leads the grace.

"All look unto thee, O Lord; and thou givest them their meat in due season; that thou givest them they gather: thou openst thine hand, and they are filled with all things in abundance." He looks up. "Amen."

"Amen."

"Amen."

We start to eat. Nelson makes conversation. He gets right to the point, stabbing right to it, without passion or interest. "So Benjamin. I was sorry to hear of your Professor's suicide. That must have been quite traumatic."

"Oh. Yeah. It was." What else could I say?

"Nelson," Stacey chides him for his lack of tact. He raises his hand apologetically.

I don't want a fuss. "No, it's alright. I mean. Have to accept what it is."

Awkward silence.

Nelson offers the bottle. "More wine, my dear?"

"I better not," Stacey reluctantly declines. "I'm still on call."

"Geez, I don't know how you can do that. Must be so stressful."

"Hard work is the touchstone of a virtuous life, Benjamin," Nelson tells me, "We're not all philosophy majors and paragons of nepotism."

"Nelson!" Her rebuke is stronger this time, but I can't actually contradict anything he said.

Nelson apologetically half-shrugs again, but his passive-aggressive tone is apparent. I don't mind. After months of sympathy, it's actually refreshing to be called out on something, earned or otherwise. Yet I can't let them know I appreciate it.

So I challenge. "Well, how's your job Nelson?"

"It's rewarding on its own merits." He smiles warmly and holds Stacey's hand. "More so is the satisfaction of providing for my family."

"Aww," my sister coos.

I look at them again with that same admiration and a tinge of pain. I wish I had that. It seems so distant, so foreign. Yet there it is. People all over the world, every day.

Nelson warms up too. Stacey has that effect.

"You're family too, Ben. It's good that we're all together."

"*Storge* right back at you, brother-in-law."

"What's that?"

"*Storge*. It means affection, particularly in the familiar sense. It's one of The Four Loves."

"Was that a Doo-Wop group?" Stacey asks, and we all laugh.

"No, it's C.S. Lewis. He articulated the concept based on ancient Greek thinking."

"Can you really quantify love like that?" Stacey asks.

"I'm not sure *quantify* is the right word."

"Analyze then."

"Well I've never understood romance," I admit.

"Ha!" Nelson enjoys that.

"At any rate, I'm glad we're a family." Stacey smiles.

COX FARMS

Cox Farms is a huge pumpkin patch/Halloween farm/family attraction. They have a corn maze, slides, farmer's market, haunted hayride, and plenty of apple cider. It is a brisk fall day as we walk through. I am filled with the warmth of nostalgia and the exhilaration of new romance. Winona is happy to be with me, affectionately amused at my childlike awe.

"I used to come here all the time with my family," I tell her.

"Not ALL the time," she points out.

"Once an October, to be precise. You know, pumpkin season."

Winona looks around. "And you have fond memories of this place, well into your college years?"

"Grad school years," I correct, making her point stronger.

"Talk about holding on."

"Come, come Winona. You of all people know the draw of nostalgia."

"Sure do."

"Freshly squeezed cider, my dear?"

I walk over to a picnic table, where there are huge orange jugs of apple cider, and stacks of little paper cups.

Also yellow-jackets. A lot of them. Swarming around the cider.

"And get stung to pieces by a horde of wasps? Nice try!'

I take a cup. "They're actually yellow jackets." I stroll over to the big orange jug. "And as you can see..." I pour (squeeze?) myself a cup and drink, satisfied. Unstung. "...They're mostly harmless."

Winona approaches, curious. "What's the deal?"

I hand her a cup. "Probably too busy feasting on that sweet, sweet apple nectar themselves to concern themselves with the skin of man."

She accepts the cup and takes a sip. "Oh."

"Right?"

"Wow." She's pleased.

"Freshly squeezed. All you want, for free."

"This place ain't bad." She sees the slides. They are surprisingly steep. "Are those slides where they sit on a burlap sack and ride down an absurd length?"

"Indeed."

She loves it. "This is awesome-sauce!"

She set me up. I gesture to a pot of spiced applesauce, over a fire. "This is applesauce."

We walk through the pumpkin patch, cups of cider in hand, looking at various pumpkins.

"We didn't really do the whole jack-o-lantern thing," Winona tells me. "Not really."

"Oh?" I cherish any insight into her past. "Do secular Jewish families not celebrate Halloween?" I guess that wasn't a serious question.

"No. We do. And I loved it. Obviously. Look at me! Just that we always used this plastic light-up pumpkin from Walmart. So you can use the same one, year after year."

"Did you also use one of those plastic pumpkins for trick or treating?"

"Hell no. A pillowcase can hold much more loot."

A 4-year-old comes running up, his harried parents behind him.

"Whoa, 'scuse me." Winona has to step out of the tyke's way.

He ignores her. Looks out at the sea of pumpkins. "Which ONE do I pick?!"

His father looks out at the pumpkins, bored to be here. "Oh God."

"They're all the same, sweetie," his mother insists. "Just pick one."

I feel a twinge of whimsy. Was I ever like that, when we lived on this coast, when we came here for our Halloween ornaments? I feel like my parents were more enthused. Stacey too.

This little guy. The pumpkin is the most important thing in the world. Remember that?

I step in. "That depends, buddy. You looking for a scary Jack-O-Lantern, or a goofy one?"

"Scary!" he empathically answers.

"Well let's see what we can find."

And we go into the patch, seeking the one perfect specimen capable of being molded into any manner of All Hallows Scream. I miss that. I remember when Halloween was about the candy and the scary stories, the creepy costumes and the cartoons. Somewhere along the way, it became about drinking a lot and staring at the sexy girls. What happened?

I am aware that Winona is watching me with admiration as I help the little kid find his pumpkin. That's not why I'm doing this.

I chase Winona, laughing, through the corn maze.

I help Winona up onto the hay truck, which is full of eager kids and their families excited for the ride.

The truck driver preps his passengers. "Alright everybody, I'm Logan. I'll be your Captain, and your Scarecrow today." He puts on a scarecrow's hat and gets inside the driver's seat. He has a loudspeaker mic. He puts on a scratchy, high-pitched voice. "If you eat my corn, I'll eat you!" replicating, I assume, what a scarecrow sounds like. "So get ready for a Spook-Tacular time!" And the puns. Of course.

The ride commences.

"And on your left- that's your left- you'll see the graveyard. A cautionary tale for those of you who dare to go ahead- you just might lose it!"

The "graveyard" is a plot of fake headstones, each with pun-filled epitaphs.

"Here lies Lester Moore," Winona reads. "4 slugs from a .44. No less. No more."

"This is the grave of Harry Fred," Logan announces. "Once was here, now he's dead."

Two paths diverge at a fork in the road. One leads to a sunny, well-cleared path. The other to the dark and deliberately brambly woods.

Logan stops the truck. "Alright. It's choice time people. The moment of decision. Two roads diverge in a wicked wood, and it'll make all the difference." I privately wonder how many of the kids will get that reference. "So what do you say?" Logan does a sweet, chipper voice. "Pleasant Path?"

Some of the people in the ride, including some of the kids say "Yeah!", "Pleasant Path!", etc.

Logan's voice takes on a booming, sinister quality. **"Or The Wicked Woods!"** Cheers for The Wicked Woods, including some of the children. "Wicked Woods it is!"

Winona grins big.

"Mind the cobwebs..." Logan warns, "and the goblins...and the werewolves..."

Winona pokes me.

"...and the snakes, witches, ghosts...well, watch out!

The hayride passes a Witch's House.

"And coming up, The Witch's Lair. So be very quiet everyone, because we don't want to..."

A witch pops out and cackles, startling some of the children.

"Ooh, she's a nasty one! Don't wanna get on her bad side."

Winona turns to me. "So. Is this place just as good as you remember?"

I think. Answer truthfully. "It's different. I- I had all these memories of coming here as a kid, with my family. But we stopped going. I never forgot it. But this? It's like..." I trail off. You can't recapture the past. That's true. And yet...

She's curious. "No, what?"

"Like I'm making new memories."

"Am I a part of them?

I smile as I put my arm around her. Completing the gesture, like a real, grown-up couple, she settles into me. This is it.

The hay-wagon emerges from the Wicked Woods. Now we are riding by a cornfield. There are cut-outs of various monsters and Halloween figures. It's a mix of generic monsters and appropriate pop culture references, like Jack and Sally from *The Nightmare Before Christmas*. There's also a Frankenstein's monster, a werewolf, and some Winona-like monstrosities.

Winona beams at seeing the cut-outs."

"My monsters!" she proclaims in joy.

NELSON

I sit at the table across from Nelson, who has a borderline manic expression, but cold and calm.

"Late shift," he states simply, to explain Stacey's continued absence and thus our discomfort.

Dead air. Our dynamic is not great. "Maybe we could play a game..." I then add, "until she gets back", acknowledging that our time spent together is obligatory and any "fun" would be nominal at best.

"A game." He chews the word, as if trying to wrap his head around the concept.

"Parcheesi? Words Against Humanity? Clue?" Heck, why not Twister? Could you imagine this guy? Does he relish the awkwardness, or does it just come naturally to him?

"With just the two of us."

"I don't know."

He moves to less trivial matters. "Perhaps the philosophy grad would be interested in something more cerebral."

This could be something. "Like a thinking puzzle." Nelson nods. "I remember one. You were a farmer who had a chicken, who had a bag of seed, who had a fox and who had a very small boat. Stop me if you've heard this one."

I had, so I did. "Yeah, I think I remember that one."

"One across the river at a time. Can't leave chicken alone with seed. Can't leave fox alone with chicken."

"Right. I think you have to realize that it's possible to take an empty boat across the river.

"Oh, we figure it out in the end, of course. But what of the conclusion? What happens next? The success in securing all three items in your store is surely temporary. Because that chicken will eat that seed, and that farmer will eat that chicken. Futility itself, a delaying of only one possible outcome for want of a larger boat. But why the fox? Why must a chicken farmer own a beast who will only try to eat his chickens? The total depravity of the fox cannot be ignored for the unconditional election of the chicken, whom at least gets her bag of feed and the efficacious grace extended to her in the honor of feeding her God. For even the bag of seed has its purpose to serve." I am already lost. He adds some biographic back-story, by way of explaining his viewpoint. "My parents were Calvinists. New Reformed. The conundrum that puzzles me now is the dilemma of the farmer who bit off more than he could chew in a boat that could fit only one. I am given to wonder, are we that feed, are we that chicken? Both would be more acceptable in the farmer's eyes than the unthinkable alternative, that we are, without use or meaning, The Fox on The Other Side of the River."

Chicken feed and Calvinism. Ponder that. "So does that mean we're...damned?"

"It means we have nothing to do." He is plainspoken, not bleak.

"I know the feeling."

"Don't be glib, Ben," he scolds. "I'm speaking existentially. I'm not talking about your quarter-life crisis California ennui tripe."

How to respond to such vested disdain? "Tripe?" This could get unpleasant, so thank God we're saved.

•   •   •   •   •

The door opens. Stacey is home. After a long shift of work, she grins and is revitalized to see her husband.

Nelson is just as thrilled. He gets up and she jumps into her arms.

I'm a little uncomfortable by all this physical affection around me.

Stacey notices. She gets down and takes out her wallet.

"Ben." Friendly. "Why don't you go see a movie?"

Sure, I can go see a movie. I get the picture.

I walk through the suburbs of Chicago. Hands in my pockets. Wind chilling my arms. Unsure of myself. Slightly depressed.

I end up seeing *Pixels*, a cute Adam Sandler movie where he and his friends, 1980s arcade gamers who have grown up, have to lead the fight against an alien invasion manifesting itself like the games they excelled at so long ago. Talk about Space Invaders. It's an acceptable and pleasant distraction for a couple of hours. I always liked Adam Sandler. The movie's been out for a while and there are only three other people in the theater. That's fine. There's a sense of privacy in the darkened theater which I appreciate.

How about those Calvinists? I guess in this day and age, Nelson might be a practicing Presbyterian, like J. Edgar Hoover. Predeterminism. What a trip. This Catholic always had to admit it made a certain sense. Start with the idea of an all-knowing God. A God who knows everything that will ever happen. Knows what you will do, before you do it. What you will choose before you choose it? Then what kind of choice is that? Free will is a tricky business.

Unconditional Election vs Total Depravity. Am I the fox or the chicken? Such a troubling idea to wrap your head around. God picking the winners and the losers. Who's saved and who's damned? Why would an all-loving God create someone he knew would burn in eternal hellfire? Were we playing with loaded dice? And for the love of God, tell me why he created Lucifer!

Well. It's not really such thorny theological issues getting me down.

I look across the street at Nelson and Stacey's in which things are going on.

•   •   •   •   •

Winona and I walk up to her aunt's house. Another cold night. An eventful one, as it will prove.

"It was kickass," Winona says of the film we just saw.

I agreed but was cautious to temper my enthusiasm. "One could make the argument it wasn't very feminist."

"Nah," she brushes off such bourgeois complaints. "I love Frank Miller, whores notwithstanding. He's just...he does his own thing, you know? Uninhibited. He has fun with himself. He doesn't care what they say. He's free."

I smile. "I'm glad you enjoy it." I nod, as one final punctuation. Time to say goodnight. "Well..."

Winona grabs my wrist. "Hey." She smiles warmly, with the suggestion of suggestion.

"Hey," I repeat, trying not to show my discomfort. Parting is such sweet sorrow, they say, but at the end of a date, there's this lingering uncertainty about how to end things, especially with the elephant in the room being what it is.

"You wanna come in?" There it is.

I put my hands in my pockets, as if that will in any way alleviate this unbearable awkwardness. "Well it it's pretty late." I stumble for an excuse. Maybe I can be considerate. "Don't want to wake up-"

"Aunt Tilly's out of town," she helpfully corrects.

I rub the back of my head, nervous. "It's late for me, you know. The buses..."

"I can give you a ride back." She then adds fatalistically, "if you need it."

"If you're not tired..." I attempt weakly.

"Come on." She thinks of something. An innocuous pretense. "Oh! I can show you *Deadly Knights*!"

That does it. "*Deadly Knights*?"

We sit on her bed, looking at various comic books. I am engrossed in said *Batman/Punisher: Deadly Knights*.

"Wasn't there an earlier one?" I ask.

"Yeah. *Lake of Fire*. But it wasn't that good. It was after Knightfall, so the Batman The Punisher teams up with is Jean-Paul Valley. Which makes the whole thing kinda pointless, 'cause Azrael kills anyway."

"So you don't get the ideological clash."

Winona gestures for me to hand it to her. She flips though the book. She stops when she comes to a certain page. She smiles.

She holds it up so I can see the spread. The Punisher holds a gun to The Joker's head.

"That looks like it could be the greatest moment in comic book history..." I say reverently as Winona kisses the image and sets it down. "But I bet Batman shows up and ruins it." Such is the way of the world.

Winona takes hold of my wrist. Looks me in the eye. "Hey."

"Hey."

"Do I really have to ask every time?"

She doesn't. She leans in and kisses me.

We start to make out.

I'm always unsure what to do with my hands. I have them on her back, awkwardly placed, rubbing slightly. I never want to take liberties, even though she wants me to. So do I, for that matter, certain liberties, but never the big one.

She looks down at my left hand. She takes it and puts it on her breast.

"Sweet," I say, imaging the reaction of a nerd in a teen sex romp. Perhaps irony is the last line of defense. How can something that feels so good on so many levels be so frightening, so sinful, so uncomfortable?

Making out continues. I partake of her scent. Drink of her lips. Our tongues rub together.

She pushes some of the comic books out of the way.

"I'm gonna..." she explains as she crawls over to get on my lap.

I mumble the next half-heartedly, as if thinking out loud. "That might not be the most comfortable place to sit right now..."

But she knows. She knows exactly why, and she doesn't care. That's her intention, the unbearably pleasurable yet frustrating pressure of her weight on my lap. I can't help grinding against her a little. Part of me, a beastly part of me, hopes to end the whole thing in that manner, so as to clear my head, alleviate the pressure, poach the elephant, and call it a night.

She takes off her shirt, revealing her bra. Creamy white in black lace. We continue to kiss, and I fondle, cherishing her warm softness.

Winona stops. A mixed expression on her face. Something is different this time, and, as I will see, both frightening and monumental. She nods, having made her decision.

"Ok," she says simply.

She hops off, stands up. Paces around. Trying to think how to put this. I feel dread, even as I am so aroused.

"So." Typically so confident, so in control, Winona is curiously awkward herself right now. "This is presumptuous on two levels. And the second presupposes the first- or seeks to contradict it, or um..."

She shakes her head. Walks across the room. Goes through her purse.

"Second presumption:" She takes out a condom. The world falls down. I cringe. "That you didn't bring one yourself."

I look down, nodding, jaw out in attempted affable agreement. "You'd be right there."

"First presumption obviously that you wouldn't- or didn't plan to- or didn't think...that this would be the night."

I'm numb. Cold sweat. My nose burns. My stomach falls into a pit. The back of my throat fills with that acidic feeling of bile and fear. And still, my lap throbs.

"Two for two."

She comes over to me. She's not a cruel person. She knows this is scary. She's not uncomfortable like I am, of course, but she is a little bit nervous and uncertain in her approach.

"So the third- the conclusion...my proposal..."

I sigh. What can I say?

She sits next to me. She takes my hand. "Ben. It's been six months. And I've been patient. I respect you. I want to give you your time, and your space, and your choice. I also want *this*. All of this. And I want you to want it."

"I do, Winona." I try to placate her, try to show her my desperate uncertainty. "Really, I do, it's just..."

"So, what is it? Is it just the Catholic thing?"

I shift away from her. I don't want to meet her eyes. I don't want to tell her I'm afraid of losing something, because she'd be taking it, and that's not how I see her. "No...Well that, and the other stuff."

I stand up. Take a breath. Pace myself. "It's just...so big." Moments like those. I turn away from her. "It scares me."

She gets up and touches my arm. "Hey." She is such a compassionate person. "It's okay." And if there were anyone, anyone in the world...

I face her. I try. My fears are too ridiculous, my morality too set in stone. So maybe from her perspective. "And... I don't even know why you want to with me, if you think about it." She's shocked. Good. But I go on. "I wouldn't be any good. I wouldn't know what I'm doing, or what I should do. I probably wouldn't find the- and I *know* I would..." I mouth the word "come". "Way too soon! So, what's the point? You'd be frustrated and I'd be embarrassed."

I think I made a pretty good case. But she responds with a warm, gentle laugh, as though all of my concerns are trifles, that I don't have to worry, not with her. "Ben! It's okay! Nobody's good the first time. But you get better and I'll be here to show you."

I want to believe her, and probably I do. "Would you? 'Cause I feel like...I'm just worried that I'll be awful, and you'll see that about me, and you'll like me less, or...something." But who am I trying to convince?

"Do you really think I'm that kind of person?" she asks firmly, with a hint of offense.

"No. Of course not. I, I don't know. We've done so much together."

"Everything but," she responds dryly.

Maybe I've deserved that. "Thank you. And you've gotten to know me. In every way. I opened myself up to you. Like nobody else. I really have. I love what we have. And I love you."

She likes to hear me say that, but she can't hide her disappointment. "Just not that way."

It hurts. I take her hands. "In every way. I have *Eros* for you, Winona. Four Loves? That's romantic, and I don't give that out to anyone."

"Doesn't Eros mean ero-tic?"

"It's...more than that." I don't want to be here right now. I wish I was a thousand miles away.

"Don't you want to?" she pleads, "Aren't you attracted to me?"

I touch her face gently. "You're the most beautiful woman I've ever touched."

"So, *touch* me," she insists.

I hesitate. "I...can't."

Winona breaks away from me. She's desperate, frustrated. "Why not?! Ben, I love you too. And this is very important to me. I want to share it with you. Yeah, you have to let your guard down. But that's the point! We do it together."

I don't have an answer. She storms around the room. She's done pleading. It's not going to happen. Now she's just mad.

"God, Ben, how is this supposed to make me feel?! Cause I don't like putting it all on the line and getting dumped on like this!"

The last thing I wanted. "I'm not-"

"I'm feeling pretty rejected right now, and that is NOT fun!"

It was the last thing I wanted. So, I'm getting a little mad myself. I didn't want this. I feel awful. This was so uncomfortable, and now I have to feel guilty on top of it?

"Well who asked you to put this all on me?! We've been doing fine without it! Who says we have to bring that in?!"

"I! I do!" She corrects, "I mean, we!"

I get apologetic again. I wish I could explain it in a way that made sense to her. "Please. You have to understand."

She sighs, resigned. "I don't."

There it is. I nod.

"Could you hand me my shirt?"

I give it to her. "I think I should go," I swallow.

"Yeah," she says it without passion or comment.

I kiss her on the cheek, but she doesn't look at me.

"I'll, uh, see you tomorrow."

"Sure." Her hollow words ring in me.

I head for the door, but I can't leave it like that.

"I'm sorry." A fruitless apology. So futile, so agonizing, so tragic.

Winona looks up at me. She stands up and hands me *Deadly Knights*.

"You can take the comic." I take it, unsure of the subtext. She turns away from him. "I already know how it ends."

I take one last lingering look at her, then walk out.

I shut the door behind me. Walk out of the house.

Onto the street, into the cold night holding no answers.

Under the street light, I look up at the dark house. Lower my head.

Ladies and gentlemen of the jury, what's to be done with this Benjamin Carter?

First of all, what does he want? Really?

Well, I am straight, obviously. Red-blooded heterosexual adult male, 23 years old and physically aroused when the night previously described occurred. There's no ambiguity there. I'm attracted to women, I lust after their bodies, can't help but stare, enjoy touching them when and where I'm allowed. So that's clear.

If, however, we define heterosexual as a man who wants to have sex with women, then we run into some confusion. Unmistakably, part of me does want to. The baser, animal, sinful part of me. The way of nature.

The way of grace, on the other hand, and the greater part of my rational mind and moral will, falls perfectly in line with Rome, in that I recognize that premarital relations are innately sinful, and I try to hold myself to that standard.

So, it wouldn't quite be accurate to say I "want" to fornicate then. There is a war within me, as I suspect there is in the hearts and bodies of all dutiful Christian men. As demonstrated by my above refusal, painful though it was, and continued abstinence well into my 20s, I think is clear that, whatever my instincts might be, the fact that when presented with the rare opportunity I had abided by my virtue (And look how that turned out!), goes to show the greater part of me did not and does not genuinely desire such activity.

We are all sinners though.

Truthfully, I had gone "further" than I should have, in terms of physical affection. There is no gray area with The Lord, but the precise boundaries in terms of forbidden touch has not been articulately defined by The Church. Hugs and hand holding are safe as houses. Pecks on the cheek are absolutely fine. On the lips? I guess so, but it would probably be best to keep that as a greeting, hello and goodnight. Once you get into making out, or "necking" as they used to say, you run the risk of feeding your lust, misappropriating the sexual faculty, God's gift, to be used in marriage only, in circumstances "love giving and life giving" as Mrs. Murphy at St. Christopher's taught us.

But how often does that happen? What percentage of sexual encounters perfectly fulfill such incredible standards?

Well I had strayed. The kissing was far too French, and my blood got too hot. "Second Base", to put it crudely, was certainly a sin. And that same carnal part of me wanted more, wanted third, wanted to put my tongue between her thighs. I wanted to find her 12 o'clock and make her climax. Yet even in that sinful fantasy I never imagined going all the way. The thought terrified and repelled me.

And marriage? Children? The only acceptable circumstances and the natural outcome of the act? I was a million miles away from thinking about that.

So what to do? Fornication was wrong, marriage was unthinkable, and Winona was gone.

Celibacy? No. I do want to be with someone, romantically. Not just as friends either. I wanted a girlfriend.

•   •   •   •   •

But who could I date? I know this all makes me sound like some stuffy, out-of-touch Puritan, but I'm realistic. I know everybody's doing it. Always have. That's what adults do. I've had a couple dates since I moved to Los Angeles. Even a pseudo-relationship, which I won't go into now. She broke it off after three dates, after guessing my secret. Asked me point blank. Well, through text...

I've considered joining a Catholic dating site. But I realized that the good girls I'd meet there, while certainly being of upstanding moral character and everything I *should* want, weren't what I am looking for right now either. They would be interested in marriage, and they wouldn't want to make out. I was still too irresponsible and immature to want to seriously court, and still so carnal that I did want to French and fondle, and possible finger.

If I am unable to reconcile my Catholicism and my libido, what then? I don't want a life of fornication. I pursue, without a proper amount of shame, certain sensual pleasures, but I don't dare to go all the way. Half fallen, tepid hedonism. The carnality unfulfilled. I am a man without a nation. Jesus, I assume, wants me to wait, find the right woman, settle down, get married and have children. The modern way, the way of the world, would have me sleep with whom I wanted. One-night stands would be permissible and frequent encounters with your loved one would go without saying. But I didn't want that either, terrible joke of it is, exploiting our lips and hands for pleasure is no less of a mortal sin.

Would it have been different if I had actually dated in high school, if I had actually kissed a girl before I was 22 and change? But such questions seem fruitless, as well as depressing.

In *Stand by Me*, Kiefer Sutherland's Ace Merrill tells one of his fellow bullies that if he wants to get laid, he has to date Protestant chicks, as Catholic girls only go to second base. Was my dream girl then a 1950s Catholic teenager? The kind of girl whose jock boyfriend was always trying to get fresher than she wanted to allow, would provide the level of intimacy I wanted. But that's ridiculous.

So, the conundrum of the modern Catholic heterosexual. You can't have sex before you're married, marriage only comes after an extended period of dating, and you can't find a woman to date you that long if you don't put out. Finding a woman with corresponding values would be the solution, but I was still in love with Winona. She had made herself perfectly clear, leaving me perfectly confused.

All of which goes to show how dreadfully stupid poor Ben always was in matters of sex.

· · · · · ·

I sit in my car, ready to go. Stacey sits next to me, unbuckled.

"So," Stacey says. "You're really going back to her."

"I'm going back to a lot of things."

This excites her. "Are you re-enrolling?!"

"I haven't told Dad yet, but- ""-No, that's fantastic! I'm so happy for you." She means it.

"I figured it's time, and..." I drift off.

"And that's a *real* reason to go back." She puts the emphasis on "real", which offends me, as if I had some fake reason for return.

"What do you mean?" I return sharply.

"Ben." She doesn't back up. She doesn't yet articulate, because she knows I know what she means. But she's going to make me say it.

"Stacey, I love her."

"Why?" She doesn't ask with malice or arrogance. It's an honest question.

"That's a question," I say flatly.

"Fair point," she concedes, "*WHAT* do you love about her?"

How can I even begin to answer that? "Just, you know, everything. I love that she has the eyes of a werewolf queen and the pen of some dead cartoonist."

"Werewolf queen?" How could Stacey understand?

I remember glancing at Winona doodling in the lecture center.

"I loved that she never stopped drawing."

I remember Winona in the George Mason Center of the Arts Concert Hall. She goes over her musical notes. She doodles in the margins.

"Even when she switched to music."

I remember shopping for clothes with her in a thrift store.

"I loved the way she looked in black, and she always wore black."

I remember her smoking everywhere, all the time, no matter what anybody said.

"I love that she smokes...even though I shouldn't."

I remember her blowing smoke in my face while as I stare in her eyes, intrigued.

I remember laying back under a tree on campus with her. I sit against the tree, she sits against me. She shows me her Tiebreaker drawings. I run my fingers through her hair and breathe.

"I love the way her hair smells," I break from the memories for a moment of self-consciousness. I am sitting in the car with my sister. "Even if that sounds creepy."

"It doesn't," Stacey chides me.

I remember driving through the suburbs. Winona stands up through the sun roof, running her hands through the wind. I can imagine her gripping the cool air, letting it slip through her fingers like gossamer as she cheers on me to drive faster. It's illegal. It's dangerous. It's Winona.

"I love that she was fearless," I admit to Stacey, "Even when it scared me."

I remember that night in Michael's room. Michael is another douchebag, murdering Bob Dylan with Lori, Aiyshah, Winona and me in the audience. A joint of marijuana is being passed around.

Winona takes a drag and offers it to me.

I wave my hand, don't say a word.

Winona passes the joint to Aiyshah and leans her head on me.

"She never made me do anything I didn't want."

Well, there was that one thing, I realize even as I say it. But I quickly move on.

"And she introduced me to so much."

I remember one day in the lecture center before class. I am going over the lesson plans. Which is difficult as Winona is distracting me, sitting on the desk and holding up a book of Edward Gorey's illustrations.

Also, though her black skirt isn't extremely short, my vantage point makes it quite a view.

I smile as she points to one particularly gruesome and Victorian illustration.

"Like Edward Gorey."

One night, in the living room of Winona's aunt's house, we play strip-Monopoly with Aiyshah, Agatha, Lori, Michael and Holden.

Holden is decked out in his full Marine Dress Blues, fully clothed, and with a stack of Monopoly money, deeds, and various articles of other people's clothes at his feet. He hasn't lost a glove.

Winona though, is in the process of taking off her shirt. She hands it to me, as I just got Atlantic.

"And Strip-Monopoly."

I cringe in the present, once again. Not the kind of thing to tell your sister.

"Ooh, sorry. I probably shouldn't have recounted that."

"Never apologize for your love," Stacey insists, sincere. "Any of it." I've convinced her. "You're too good."

I appreciate her saying this. Stacey really does care about me. It is important to get her perspective. Her concern comes from a good place. I know that. She asks questions I need to hear, even if I don't want to. I'm lucky to have people like that in my life. We don't always see eye to eye, and I certainly don't get her and Nelson, but in the end, you've got to stay close to the ones you have, especially when everything seems so far apart.

LEXINGTON

I am at the fabulous Clarion Hotel in Lexington, Kentucky. I sit in the lobby, holding that same fateful comic book from that one deadly night. Its pages are worn and the edges are frayed. I've read this many times, retraced the course of events. It's never as exciting as the first time, but maybe you learn a little more. What if things had turned out differently? What if Batman had put aside his code for just one time, or if The Punisher hadn't waited one more second to pull the trigger? What if they had just gone through with it? Would the joke be over?

"Sir?"

I look up. Sunny, the concierge, is ready for me.

"Can I help you?"

I approach the counter. "Hi. Hello. I've got a room for the night. It's under Ben Carter. Because that's my name." I joke, but it doesn't land. "That's Carter with a C-A"

"Gotcha!" Sunny smiles, perky. "So, what brings you to Lexington, Mr. Carter?

"I suppose the curvature of the Earth. It's between Chicago and Nashville."

"Very good."

Back on a rock in the middle of the sea. Lexington is just as isolated as the desert, or Los Angeles. All these places, so far away.

A little later, I am on the phone, calling someone who will not pick up, leaving a message that may go unheard.

"I've been...all around the country."

I look out the window of my hotel room, down at Lexington. It's a nice little city. Tucked away in Kentucky, an unassuming moderately sized state in the not so deep South.

"I'm sorry I won't make it out to see you." But what good is this apology? It's given out of obligation, without passion but not without regret. "I'm not going that far."

At The Sports Page Bourbon Bar, I sit alone, nursing a Mint Julep, appropriately as the TV shows highlights of the day's horse race. I think about that phone call I will be making when I'm in my room, before I retire. I will say:

I saw Stacey. She's doing good. She and Nelson seem really happy. I don't think he likes me very much, but that's not...

I see a happy couple at a table. She has red hair and has bright teeth, which you can see a lot because her boyfriend keeps making her laugh. He's a gregarious type, broad-shouldered, short haircut. Probably played football in high school. Who do you think they are?

I think about these things. How did they meet?

He takes her hand and she grabs it, interlocking her fingers with him and swinging, even though they are just sitting. Sitting at a little high table in a bar in a hotel, and they make it special.

How long have they been together? How long will they stay? Maybe I could ask them what Stacey asked me, ask them why they love each other. Have they had problems?

He whispers something in her ear. She smiles, looking down, coy. They're so happy it hurts me.

I want to ask them so many things. I want to go over and start a conversation and learn everything they have to teach me. Our lives are so different.

But I just sit at the bar and keep my questions to myself.

It's 9:27, approximately half an hour before the indoor pool closes. I walk along the side, looking down at its surface.

I'm in Lexington tonight. Tomorrow I'm going to Nashville. See an old college buddy. I hope he's okay.

I sit down at a pool chair next to a man with glasses watching his kids swim. He nods at me. I nod back.

I hope you're okay too.

I take off my shoes. The air is rich with chlorine. I've always liked that smell. It reminds me of hotels and road trips.

We don't talk as much as I like.

I get in the pool and start to swim. Lap after lap. It's a little like falling asleep. The water cools me, just as it numbs me, and everything feels okay.

Hair still wet, I stand in front of the vending machines, trying to make a choice.

I've been asking a lot of people for advice.

The man from the pool approaches behind me.

"Try the 'Wild' Cherry Pepsi", he advises. He smiles and makes a power fist. "If you're feeling feisty."

Goofy. Dad humor. I love it. I grin and take The Wild Cherry Pepsi.

• • • • •

I walk down the hall, Wild Cherry Pepsi on top of a full ice bucket. It's too late for such caffeine, but that advice was too good to turn down.

I'm going to see Winona again. I hesitate. I've told this person about Winona. *I don't know what I'm going to say.*

I talk on the phone as I pour my Pepsi. The cool brown soda falls on the ice in mist form, then bubbles up and settles.

"I'd really like to know what you think. I know you never met her, but..." But what?

I take a sip of Pepsi, rocking the cup, the way I used to pretend I was drinking scotch when I drank ginger ale on the airplane as a kid. I sit on the bed.

"Anyway, if you hear this, if you get a chance, if you want..." I should just end it now. "...call me back." I sigh. "I love you Mom."

I put the phone down and lie back on the bed.

DR. MODINE

"Are you sleeping any better?"

Dr. Modine is a calm, sensitive psychologist, I am in his office, and he is currently doing most of the talking.

I shrug. "Should I be?"

"You need the rest," Dr. Modine assures me. "If it becomes a problem, I could prescribe something."

My mind wanders. "Like Nyquil?"

"Something stronger. More effective."

"Good." I decide to open up. Not really. Not about what he really wants me to talk about. But I can tell him something. "Because Nyquil is one of the 4 Most Depressing Things I Know."

He doesn't comment on the list, but he does ask, "Why?" Tries to wrap his scientific mind around it. "Granted, it does have a small alcoholic content, but overall it's nowhere near the depressant that say, beer is."

He doesn't get it. Why would he? "Well I'm not even sure if this is true, but if it is, it's definitely on my Top 4. I was talking to one of my friends once, and he told me that if you really want to fall asleep fast, chugging Nyquil is not the best way to go-"

"-Oh, definitely not." The good doctor is quick to agree with this diagnosis.

"-Because if you drink too much, it will keep you up!" I finish that sentence perhaps a little louder and more manic than I should.

David Dawes and I were talking about insomnia one night. Late night study session in the library. David said it idly, like a point of fact carrying no specific significance or emotional investment to him. I mean, he made it sound like he had tried it in the past, but no big deal.

But YES big deal! I was going to have to explain why.

"It's true that in excessive doses-" But I cut him off.

"And that's what sucks about it! Like a guy is tired- he's just trying to get to sleep! And he's desperate. So he knows about Nyquil. He knows that's supposed to be a sleep aid. And doc, he REALLY wants to sleep. Like right now. So he chugs a lot. But it DOESN'T help! It backfires! It keeps him up!" I was near tears. I had to calm down. I finished weakly. "All he wanted was to sleep..." It just doesn't seem fair.

Dr. Modine is patient, and rather than comment on the alarming nature of my outburst, kindly addresses its content, explaining. "Nyquil contains Dextromethorphan, which consumed in large quantities can actually inhibit the serotonin conducive to sleep. Like I said, not the best method."

So, there that is. A scientific explanation for the grievance of a tantrum the good doctor was magnanimous enough to treat as legitimate. Top 4 Most Depressing, Ben? There's cancer. There's AIDS. War. Orphans. And I'm crying about Nyquil?

I don't have an answer to that. The matter seemed resolved. I wasn't trying to get pills or anything. And really the question "Are you sleeping any better?" implies that the issue that sent me here in the first place was keeping me up at night. It isn't. No more than usual, anyway. I've had difficulty sleeping since middle school, but it isn't chronic, isn't caused by Wilkinson blowing out his brains in front of me, and it isn't the main problem.

What is? I feel uncomfortable in Dr. Modine's office, uncomfortable in my own skin. Not because of him. He's a nice guy, and probably as compassionate, comforting and warm a shrink as you could find.

The problem is me. I feel like a fraud. Like I'm only here out of obligation. People know what you witnessed- they don't know what it's like, but they figure, it must have messed you up. You should talk to somebody. So I am going through the motions, but it isn't helping, and (worse?), I worry I don't need help. Is it bad I'm not more upset? I cried a couple times, it hurts my stomach to think about, but...I am functioning. I know people would tell me I am suppressing, I am holding back, and maybe I am. But what can I do? Where is the catharsis? There's no "It's not your fault" scene here. I'm going through the motions of grief everyone said I should, but it feels fake, and I don't know if that is good or bad. I just don't know.

There is an awkward silence, and then Dr. Modine gets to the more serious concerns.

"So," he says matter-of-factly, "You're dropping out."

When I came in, I noticed that today, Dr. Modine had on his desk, of all things, a Rubik's Cube. I didn't ask permission to pick it up and play with it, because I know he would immediately smile and say "Sure!" or "Knock yourself out!" with a sickening and very real affability, followed by a disgraceful self-effacing remark like "Could never get more than a side on that damn thing myself!" It is all so predictable, so safe. Makes me want to roll my eyes and puke.

So I pick it up without permission, even though it was assumed, because really, I don't want permission. Everyone is so nice these days. I hate it.

"Wouldn't you?" I say flatly, dryly. Maybe I'll walk out of his office with this stupid thing. Not that I was any good at it. And I would feel guilty.

He gives a conceding, non-committal nod. "I would be tempted. It's a lot to deal with."

"A lot." I'm exhausted. "I...I just can't."

"Ben, nobody's expecting you to go right back into it. That wouldn't be fair. You need some time. You've had a traumatic experience. I just want you to know, you're not alone. People care about you, and they're there for you. You family, your friends..."

Family. Friends. Absent mother? Suicidal professor? Ex-girlfriend?

"-She left!" I snap. The good doctor waits. I calm myself. "She's in Europe." I don't want to talk about Professor Wilkinson. But as long as I have an ear, I can whine about Winona. "And yeah it happened before- before...But all at once? That's not supposed to happen. Break-up, then this."

"It's so much," he agrees.

"So why should I go back to school?"

He's delicate. "It's hard. You need to take your time. And it's understandable if you find George Mason...tainted somehow. If you need a change of climate."

"California. My Dad's giving me a job. Out in Los Angeles."

"Good," he smiles. "Now that's a change of climate!"

"Yeah. Santa Monica."

"Wow!" Now comes that unbearable cheeriness. "Sunshine. Beaches. You're getting me jealous. It may surprise you, but I used to be quite the surfer."

"Oh yeah?"

"Yeah, back in the day. I saw 'The Endless Summer' when I was a kid. Got me hooked."

"Haven't seen it. Great poster though." I thought of the yellow sun, orange sand, pink sky. Silhouettes of the surfers approaching the horizon. When I was a kid, I would see the box in the video store. It intrigued me, especially the word endless. Made it seem mythic.

He agrees about the poster. "Oh, EVERY guy had that one in my dorm." He sighs. "Yeah, if you tried to put me on a board today...well, my wife would veto it, of course, and the waves on the East Coast-"

"I was there. I was there and I watched and I did nothing." Might as well make an effort. Might as well say what you're supposed to.

He shifts from surfing to suicide without losing a beat. "There was nothing you could have done. If you had tried to take the gun, he could have shot you. You couldn't talk him out of it. That's not on you."

Here it comes. Maybe I do need to hear that. Maybe "It's not your fault" is real, and necessary. Maybe I'm here for a reason.

I'm near tears. "This didn't just happen."

"Ben, it wasn't your fault. There's no way you could have predicted it. Mark was sick."

"That's what we think!" I go another, more unthinkable route. "But the one thing that's gotten me worked up, more than ANYTHING about this is- WHAT IF...he was right?!" Dr. Modine patiently deals with this digression. I try to explain what I'm getting at, even if I don't know myself. "I mean. We all go around, EVERYONE thinks they've figured it out. He said he did. That he understood the universe. I mean how do we know he wasn't right? To us he was just another crackpot, but how do we know he wasn't right? What if HE was the one who figured it out? What if he's in some dimension right now, or Nirvana, or that state of godhood he was talking about?"

And I meant that question. You meet a homeless woman at the bus stop. Try to be nice. Start up a conversation and five minutes later she's ranting about demons and energy. You think she's crazy, feel sorry for her. Because you know how the universe works. Because you're normal and sane, and she's not. And you're probably right. And yet...

"I can't attest to the validity of delusions. There's nothing there."

"Yeah, but why?! Sick? Like what, he just has bad chemicals or something?"

"The human brain is a complex organism, and in all honesty, there's still so much about it we don't know. We can prod and prick under a microscope, but even if we were able to fully scope the physical mechanisms of the organ itself, you might still wonder about that elusive, nebulous concept we call the mind. It's not something they teach you in medical school, and it's not something you can quantify, if it can even be said to exist. Your brain's not a prison for your soul, because you are that. People don't like to think that their actions, their will, is all just a function of a series of chemical reactions. It's not a comforting thought. But what are thoughts? Listen. I'm not an anatomist, I'm not a neurologist, and I'm certainly not a philosopher. When I psychoanalyze your thoughts, I can't truly say I know where they're coming from, or why. But that doesn't mean I can't help."

This both leaves me in the cold while simultaneously comforting me. I feel cold and alone that this doctor I am talking to is clearly not a Christian, that he inhabits a positivist universe without a God, a dead, mostly empty space just awaiting its inevitable heat death.

At the same time, he was open about the fact that he didn't have the answers. He's approachable, and he's approaching me. He's making an earnest attempt to help me. And I...

I nod, trying to get past it. "Thanks," I breathe in. "Thank you. I'm sorry I was being difficult." I don't like to be difficult. I don't like to disappoint people. I'm so sorry. I'm so scared. I wish they would just like me. I hate to do anything wrong.

"No, not at all," Dr. Modine assures me. He's so kind. I was wrong to be cynical. What's wrong with me?

Now my real breakdown begins, and it comes not from pining for Winona or musing about Wilkinson but takes its form in gratitude and apology to Modine. "No really, I'm sorry. You're so good. And you're just trying to help me. And you're a good man. You're helping people. Your wife made you give up surfing." I feel bad about that. "I-I-I...don't need to trouble you. You don't deserve that." I'll die if he hands me a tissue box, so I wipe my tears and take another breath. "Thank you. This has helped."

I just want him to be happy.

NASHVILLE

I drive into Nashville, another city I have never been to, another place that doesn't know me. Those clouds are warm above, and the locals are friendly. I hear good things about the food, and the music as well, though I am not here to eat.

It is a lovely two-story cabin above the city. I park and go up to knock on the door. After a moment, Kennedy opens up. She's a pretty young Irish woman, short and stout, with a lot of cute freckles and autumn red hair. A thick accent, holding one baby and incubating another.

"Hello."

She smiles warmly. "You must be Ben!"

"Which would make you Kennedy?"

"It does. This here's Margaret. She's not talking yet, but I'm sure she's pleased to meet you as I am."

Holden is outside, practicing on his personal firing range. Currently with a rifle which he aims with extreme precision, but there is a handgun on the table beside him.

We come out of the house. "Holden!" Kennedy calls.

Holden puts down to the gun. He turns and is pleasantly surprised to see me approaching. I made good time.

"Home is the sailor, home from the sea," I remind him.

"And the hunter, home from the hill," he returns, and we embrace.

"Good to see you in a Red State again," he quips.

I laugh, even though I have always hated that divisive dichotomy. "Ha, yeah. It's been quite a trip."

He turns to his wife. "Lass, let's take Ben out to the steakhouse. Get a big hot piece of meat, dripping raw into his mouth."

"Probably could be phrased better," I point out.

Kennedy loves the idea. "Oh, I'll call Jolene! It'll be fun."

I look at the assorted guns and ammo on the table. Typical Holden. But Kennedy? I turn to her, "So are you okay with all these live firearms around here, your baby-"

"-*Our* baby," she corrects. I would have to try to get answers without asking later. It was my understanding that Holden was not Margaret's father.

"-And pregnant and everything?"

Kennedy hands Margaret to Holden. He coos lovingly over the baby and she gurgles back. And he is such a deadly man.

"Ben, you've always known me to be extraordinarily cautious." That's true, and now he was looking alarmingly like a father.

Then I see why Kennedy handed over her baby. To free her hands. She picks up the handgun. Takes a shot. Bull's-eye.

• • • • • •

Stoney River Steakhouse and Grill. Rustic, and the air is full of the crisp smell of barbecue. I sit across from the McQueens (still weird), Jolene next to me. She is an attractive woman with a nose ring. She wears a white skirt and I can feel her thigh pressed against me. She works for the city, controlling radios for the police dispatch. She says it is interesting work, and that she loves cops. She will mention several times throughout the night that she hates Elvis, makes a point of it, that even though she has lived in Nashville all her life (something one could detect intuitively by that Southern tang in her voice), she should be exalted because she is not a fan of the King of Rock and Roll.

"We're thinking Bridget if a girl," Holden is telling me, rubbing his wife's pregnant stomach.

"Brian if a boy," she nudges him. "Big guy here vetoed Holden Jr."

"My intention is to dispel any notion of favoritism," Holden explains. "I already anticipate some juvenile anxieties in Margaret being that I am not her biological father." He pokes Margaret in her chubby tummy, and she gurgles affectionately.

Kennedy assures Holden, "Oh, you're the only Daddy she's ever known."

Jolene emphatically agrees, to the point of bitterness. "And Sam was a..." Kennedy covers little Margaret's ears. Jolene cleans it up. "You-know-what-hole."

Kennedy goes on. "And Holden's been a godsend." She smiles and leans on him. "My miracle with a machine gun."

"You're going to make me blush, lass."

"And he works fast!" I immediately regret this joke. "Sorry."

But I'm greeted with warm laughter.

"Irish twins," Kennedy says.

"So what did bring you to America?" I ask.

"Rosemary."

"Say again?"

"I've very infused with the home homeopathic business," she tells me. "Essential oils, incense. Scents are very soothing."

"And profitable," Holden adds. That makes sense. I wouldn't think Holden would take up with such New Age shenanigans if there weren't a more grounded angle.

Jolene turns to me. "Ben, did you know that the olfactory is the sense most connected to memory?" I think she knows it. I can smell her perfume. I wonder if Kennedy made it. Lavender. Appealing.

I try a joke. "I have heard that, and I feel it has the taste of truth."

Holden smirks, joining in. "I see what you did there."

An old classic starts to play over the restaurant's loudspeakers. Holden loves Kennedy tender, that's clear, and Margaret, and Bridget/Brian. Look at what they have.

Jolene groans. "Not again!"

Holden laughs. "Don't knock The King!"

Kennedy nuzzles Margaret. "We want to make sure she has an appreciation for the finer things in life."

I look at my friend. His new wife. New life. I think it's kind of funny, I think it's kind of sad. I feel awe and disbelief, and a tinge of whimsy.

"Wow. It's so...look at you. Home business, wife, *kids*! You're just...so grown-up. It's crazy."

"Ben," Kennedy gently corrects, "I think it's very sane."

I guess she's right. "It's just nice to see you both."

Holden smiles warmly as he takes Kennedy's hand, Margaret in his lap. "It's nice to be seen. It makes you feel real."

I nod. I know exactly what he means.

PROFESSOR SKARSGÅRD

Professor Skarsgård's home, much like the man himself, is warm and academic. So many books. Who has time to read that much? A large collection of books usually makes me feel inadequate, but now it's cozy and inviting, because the professor himself is.

I sit with Winona on the couch while the Professor is in the next room.

"I like this," I tell her. "An adult inviting us together. Like we're a real couple type thing."

She knows what I mean. She smiles, squeezing my hand.

"We are a real couple type thing."

Professor Skarsgård enters the room, jovial, carrying a tray with tea.

"Tea, babies, I brought tea."

"Aww, thanks Professor," Winona takes her cup, grateful.

"As for the music, well, I'll defer to your choices. Young people and all that."

"I appreciate the voice of confidence," I tell him, though really, my musical knowhow is nothing to sing about.

He takes a seat, sitting himself comfortably across from us.

"Are you in a band there, Ben?"

"Me?"

"No, the, uh, rock star behind you."

We all laugh.

"Ben's tone deaf in both ears."

"Hey," I'm mock defensive, "I played the recorder in third grade."

"I used to be quite the rocker myself," he says casually, as if he doesn't know this is going to get a lot of follow-up. False modesty? Humble brag? I love it.

"Shut up!" Winona is over the moon.

"It's true!"

"Wow..." I'm trying to picture this polite Scandinavian academic rocking out. It's just not coming to mind. "Why?"

That's actually a weird question to ask, now that I look back, but that's all I could think.

And he doesn't mind. He can understand why someone would ask why. After all, him? Professor Erik Skarsgård, Western Literature Chair, in a rock band?

And he has his answer ready immediately.

"Girls."

"Of course." Winona smirks.

"I joined the band for the same reason we all did: to get the girls. There's always been just something so...electrifying about the rock star, monumental. Mythic. I dare say they've become the legends of our time."

"Well I thought superheroes were quite obviously the modern-day legend."

"Superheroes aren't real, Ben," Winona reminds me.

"No, he has a point. You both do. Superman and Spider-Man are mythic, Ben. But they are fake, Winona."

So, we both got one. He goes on.

"If folk heroes are real, and now, then they are rock stars."

"Okay," I concede, because I know he's going to go on to make an excellent point, as he always does. "They are what our culture glorifies, exalts. Our Hercules in heavy metal. Samson's in a hair band. Arthur puts down Excalibur and picks up a Fender."

We laugh, but he is onto something, and he articulates himself well, as always.

"I wasn't so philosophical at the time, of course. And of course, we weren't any good. That and the fact we were dawning at the dusk of Swedish Death Metal left us no place to go. But these futile adolescent explorations instilled in me a great curiosity, the less than primrose path to where I am today. More experimental at the end of Dödåskathat, which was what we called ourselves."

"What does that mean?" Winona asks.

"I won't tell you. It's deadly..." He mock-glowers. Swedish Death Metal. I love it.

"I experimented with sampling Wagner. Because it sounded cool. After our own downfall, I explored that artist on his own terms, intellectually, in scholarly pursuit. From thence came the Ring Cycle, Germanic Mythos, Beowulf, the Rise of Western Civilizations, all the way to my present course of study, the Professor standing- sitting before you now. My point, if you're still listening..."

"Aw, we are!" Winona assures him. "This is really fascinating. Because what you're talking about, it's a process."

"A path," I agree.

"Your life's journey." She's digging it. "That's just so cool. You start rocking, and that leads you here."

"Exactly. Exactly." He's pleased she gets it. "My point is that there never exists but one path to...anything, pretty much. All roads lead to Rome, and your Rome can be anything you want it to be. Love, life, God."

I knew what Rome was to me. It was literally Rome. And that's where God was.

"The essence of Rock and Roll is exuberance, an unhindered release of the creative beast inside. Let him loose some time. You'll be surprised what prey he sniffs out, hunts, and lays down before you."

"I'll have to keep it in mind." And I will. And I do.

"Keep your nose open, pal." She nudges me. I don't know what she means by it. "Professor, I'm glad you bring up music. I'm actually switching majors."

"Again," I note, and perhaps I shouldn't have. She playfully punches me.

"Are you, my dear? That's wonderful." And then he answers that question I couldn't ask. "It's wonderful, because if you feel like switching majors, you should, because to stay somewhere you don't want to be is stifling, and that is not the point of a higher education."

"Exactly." Winona is glad he gets it.

"What arena of study are you shifting to now?"

"Music, naturally. Hence the segue."

"Oh fantastic. I've always thought you had an artistic sensibility. Your drawings are terrific, a real gothic treat. I'm sure your endeavors into the musical world will entrance us all as well."

"Aww, that's sweet. I'm just worried I'm too fluid. First, I was undeclared, then I was declared, then undeclared again, now I'm redeclared."

I rub her back, reassuredly, I hope. Now I will try to support her, like a good boyfriend should.

"Well like the man says, some people's education is a flowing river with curves and brooks and what not." I don't know why I said that. I don't know what it means or even who said it. Maybe nobody did. I'm not sure I approve of Winona's decision. I'm afraid to tell her that- though internally, I think it significant that I now feel I have a right to "approve" or "disapprove" of anything she does. Like she's mine, and what I think counts.

Maybe I should tell her.

But she's responding so well to these pleasantries, this obligatory lip-service in support of whatever she does, how ill-advised or unadvised, as it were, that I don't have the strength to ruin that beautiful smile, leaning into me now, as if we truly are that perfect adult couple type thing we talked about. I can't spoil that.

So I talk about myself.

"I guess I'm more on a set path, personally."

"And that's okay, too." Winona pats my hand. Am I being patronized?

"Ben, I understand you're studying under Mark Wilkinson."

"Ben's his TA," Winona answers proudly.

"Brilliant man." He's pleased. "Intense, but brilliant."

• • • • •

Jolene's house is comfortable and cozy, with a nice view of the woods. We have to creep in so as not to disturb her parents. We walk down the stairs to the basement where her room and the entertainment lounge is.

What am I doing here?

I try to piece together the sequence of events, but the blend of alcohol and incredulity make it hazy. I register, strictly in the academic, in the abstract, that a young woman has taken me home. Odd, I don't think I was being especially charming, but then I've never fancied myself to be an especially charming guy.

It makes precious little sense, but here I am.

"It folds out to a bed," Jolene says, pointing to the futon. "I can get some blankets."

She leaves me, I assume, to fetch said beddings. Perhaps, I think as I pull open the bed, she just means to give me a place to sleep. I am both relived and disappointed by the notion. That makes even less sense, however. Everyone knows I came to Nashville to stay with my old friend Holden. What sense would it make to send me home with an absolute stranger? Then I recall how close Jolene sat next to me in the car ride home, how she leaned into my arm and acquiesced to my drunken peck on her cheek, and it seems that sex is the only option.

"Ben, what have you gotten yourself into this time round?" I chuckle to myself as I sit on the edge of the bed, which won't quite flatten right.

"You have to pull it, up and out," she explains, coming down the stairs with a handful of blankets, seeing my physical conundrum but not my spiritual malady or moral dilemma.

"Thanks," I say as she helps me pull it, up and out, until it is spread like a bed.

"You know, I've known Kennedy since she moved here," Jolene explains, taking a seat on the bed. I feel obliged to join her. "From Ireland."

"She's really something," I say this platitude rotely, meaning little by it as I edge up on the bed and contemplate my immediate future. "They both are. I'm glad he found her."

"Definitely. Sam was an asshole."

"I wouldn't know."

"Well he was. Believe me."

"I do."

She scoots a little closer.

"I don't like to talk about all that. He left as soon as she told him. What a gentleman."

I surmise that she told him she was pregnant. The model of irresponsibility. What a cad.

"So, uh," I begin nothing especially, just registering that she doesn't like to talk about all that, "How do you like Tennessee?"

"As opposed to...?"

"Anywhere else?" I shrug.

"It's alright. We get some nice tax breaks, which is nice. It gets hot sometimes though, and the people can be backwards."

"As opposed to?"

"I don't know. New York? LA? I've never been to those places."

"I have. They're places. Geographical. People are the same all over."

"Do you really think that's true?"

"Yeah, I think I do."

"Cool," she nods noncommittally.

It occurs to me that she might be expecting me to make a move. We are here, after all.

Then a fascinating idea hits my head. What if I...did? What if I just went for it, right now? I almost laugh at what an ironic twist that would be. How deliciously anti-climactic if I were to just nonchalantly lose my virginity at this time and place? It was ridiculous of course, and yet, what if?

What if...

"Do you like music?" she asks. It's a banal question, but I welcome banality at this point.

"Well sure," I shrug, sitting back. She's taking out her iPhone and I see a speaker on the mantle. She's going to play us something. "You got any Chris Isaak?"

"Chris Isaak," she repeats flatly.

"Yeah. He's a singer."

"I know who he is. I think he played in Nashville last year. But why are you asking me about Chris Isaak?" She asks this with a blend of incredulity and disdain.

"It's a natural response given to the question asked. You asked me if I liked music. I said Chris Isaak."

"Yeah, I guess. But he seems kind of...I don't know, Mom Rock."

"Yes, um," I answer reluctantly, honestly, "My Mom's into him."

"Don't you think you're old enough to have your own taste in music?" she smirks, and I guess this was supposed to be affable, so I shrug.

"I do. I've come to appreciate him on my own."

"Why?" She had taken off her denim jacket, and I notice her bare shoulders and cleavage.

I try to think, how to describe my Serenader of Dreamland.

"Well, just listen."

"I don't have any." She stands up. "But I can do Spotify."

As she crossed the room to turn on the music, I checked her skirt. It is short, isn't it? I can make out her thighs, and I imagine it would take very little effort to crank my neck up and see more. Sometimes I hate being like this.

Wicked Game. The Greatest of Greatest Hits, and I have no complaints. I don't have to go deep tonight.

Jolene crosses the room as that familiar tortured twang starts. She sits next to me. Close. Her legs might be spread further than they should be. I distract myself by talking about the music.

World was on fire and no one could save me but you.

"He's soulful. He's been hurt. I mean, I think he has. I just experience his music, in the music, in the moment."

It's strange what desire will make foolish people do.

"His voice...it's soothing, elegant- with an edge. Masculine and feminine all at once. It takes a hold of you."

I never dreamed that I'd meet somebody like you.

"Takes you to some other place." I almost say *Dreamland,* but I return to reality so as not to weird her out. "I've seen him on stage. In San Francisco, with Dwight Yoakam. He commands the stage, and the audience follows. The way he moves, and his eyes..."

I never dreamed that I'd lose somebody like you.

"You're not some sorta a fag, are you?"

I'm taken aback by the question, but I get a perverse sort of pleasure in hearing it asked. That's not the sort of word you hear in polite society, but polite society never met Holden McQueen, and I don't think his circle runs that way either. I'm not invested enough to tell Jolene her language was offensive, and I don't think she would care either.

Part of me wants to reply, snarky but macho, "Ask me in the morning," and then throw her on the bed, "take her", lips, body, and all, as the heroic movie star lovers would do, and show her thusly my heterosexual credentials were not all academic.

But I know that's not in the cards.

No, I don't want to fall in love.

"No, I…" I'm too drunk to think of some clever reproach.

No, I don't want to fall in love.

"I have a girlfriend. Had a girlfriend."

With you.

"Yeah?" she asks, too casual and inebriated to realize how pointed her question is, "Where is she?"

What a wicked game we play, to make me feel this way.

●   ●   ●

I stay one more night with Holden. The day was a blur. I slept in at Jolene's till 12. Drank too much. She didn't mind. She dropped me off at Holden's with very little small talk. Maybe she liked me. Maybe she was doing her friend a favor. Maybe such obligations are ridiculous, and dehumanizing, and rough.

I sort of mope around that day, politely offering to help around the house with chores to Kennedy's magnanimous declinations. Holden comes back late, and then we can talk.

●   ●   ●

We sit in the back, taking in the wide and starry Tennessee night. An ocean of space above us little mites in the country.

"I'm reminded of...two books right now," Holden starts to pontificate. "*Heart of Darkness* and *The Great Gatsby*."

"Probably because of the stars, right?" I venture, "I don't know what specific reference you're making, but we're under a lot of stars."

He nods.

"'And this also, has been one of the dark places of the Earth'", he takes a somber tone.

"Time was," I agree.

"Time was, Marlow knew, before the Romans, before the Knights, and long before the Imperialists, even England herself was a dark and untamed land, a frontier of the savage unknown."

The pinpoints of light in the firmament are almost overwhelming. So close, yet so far. Those precious clouds, so comfortable and dreamy in the way, have retreated to their nocturnal resting places so that I can enjoy the majesty of the next. Such a massive night invites profound conversation.

"I guess all places were like that," I try to contribute, "Even when they crossed the Bering Strait, they had no idea what they were in for. I guess once we left the Garden of Eden, all bets were off."

"Truer words were never spoken. But consider Nick Carraway, when speaking of those first Dutch eyes to behold this brave new world: 'For a transitory enchanted moment man must have held his breath in the presence of this continent, compelled into an aesthetic contemplation he neither understood nor desired, face to face for the last time in history with something commensurate to his capacity for wonder.'"

We look up at the stars and contemplate.

"So who's right?" I ask, "Marlow or Carraway?"

"Oh they both are, of course. That's why when I look up to the stars and think of the first spacemen who will tread on distant worlds, I feel both envy, and pity. The duality of our reaction to the unknown is that curious mix of horror and wonder that simultaneously repels and enchants us."

"Fear and desire."

Kennedy comes out of the house cradling Margaret.

"Goodnight, boys."

"Goodnight, lass." Holden reaches up and kisses his baby and his wife goodnight. "Benjamin and I are just contemplating the infinite. It may take all night."

"Goodnight, Kennedy."

"You're off in the morning, then?"

"I am. Thank you for hosting me. This has been a great couple of days. That was a wonderful dinner."

"It was. I'm just sorry you and Jolene-"

Holden clears his throat.

"Yeah," I say sheepishly, "I didn't know I was supposed to..."

Supposed to what? What was expected of me?

She picks up on the awkward readings and mercifully retreats.

"Well I'll leave you boys to it. Don't be thinking too hard."

She leaves with the baby.

"Jolene was nice..." I insist, before Holden cuts to the heart of the matter.

"Yes, I suppose it is time to address the lithe, Gothic, bewitching elephant in the room."

"Three days." It's coming so soon.

"Oh Ben. Gentle Ben. Benjamin. Last Son of Israel. What's to be done?"

"I don't know."

"Ben, lesser, ignorant college fellows would either tear out their hair in incredulous frustration or think you are latent homosexual that the initial wedge in your relationship was that you would NOT have premarital sexual relations with Winona."

Yes, he knows it all. Yes, I told him everything. Perhaps more discretion would have been prudent. But he's my closest friend in this world, and I appreciate his counsel, no matter how painful it is to hear.

"That's not exactly-"

"But I understand. And I respect your reasons. Fear and Desire, your say. And virtue. That too. And Catholic Guilt. And Love, ah, love. It's a briny mix, and I don't envy you."

"I know. It's hard. But...at least it's real. I'm a part of something real." I stand up. Look into the Tennessee countryside. "Sometimes I don't know where I'm going."

"But you know where you've been."

That's right. I peer into the distance. It must be somewhere near here.

"How far are we from Gatlinburg?"

"That's the other side of the state," Holden answers, surprised at the query. "What do you want to go there for? It's nothing but miniature golf and tourist traps."

"Oh yes," I light up, remembering. "A lot of them. Ripley's Believe it or Not. The Guinness Book of World Records Museum. The Earthquake Simulator. Mirror Maze. Funhouse. Hall of Illusions. Talking Genie Ball. That whole town blew my mind when I was ten. We stopped by there on a road trip. Rented a cabin, kinda like yours."

"I doubt that," he huffs. But I'm already in the past.

"We went to all those 'tourist traps' during the day, and at night, Stacey and I slept in the living room- with the TV. Dad didn't let us have cable at home, so whenever we stayed at a hotel, or went to Granddad and Grandmom's...well, Stacey and me watched Cartoon Network 'til we fell asleep."

"That must have been in the early days."

"Yeah. *Cow and Chicken*," I answer, nostalgic.

"I liked *Johnny Bravo*," he smirks, "There's something audacious about making a children's cartoon about a guy trying to get laid all the time."

"Hah. Yeah. That was just one of the last times...I mean before Mom..."

I trail off. He gets it.

"What is it we find so comforting about nostalgia," he asks, pensive.

"Well duh. We all talk about what cartoons we used to watch, or our favorite breakfast cereals, 'cause those are happy times. We like to think about that. I mean, the future's scary."

I say this with a touch of whimsy, and, so often, regret. I recall vaguely, intellectually, that I often didn't like those road trips. Getting up early, sitting in the car for hours and hours. Camping. Yet looking back now, I could remember nothing but fondly.

Then Holden brings me back to reality.

"I'm going back to Afghanistan."

This takes another moment to register. He is matter-of-fact in his fashion, but I'm shocked.

"What?!"

"I ship out in six months."

"But you've already done two tours. Why are they making you?"

"They aren't. My choice."

I don't get it.

"You...What is this, Holden? Your bullshit Gospel of War thing again?"

"I stopped preaching that scripture," he shakes his head. "I'm thinking of the real now. What's important."

"What's important?" I protest, trying to make sense, "You've got a family now! You have a wife, and a baby, and another one on the way. How can you just..."

"Why do you think I'm going over there?" he asks simply. "Who do you think I'm fighting for? Who am I trying to protect?"

I have no politics in this conversation. I have nothing but melancholy.

Kennedy comes out of the house, holding a guitar. Holden chuckles and feigns a protest.

"Oh no, lass. Get that out of here!"

She sits in his lap and hands him the guitar.

"Not a chance, lad."

"How's my angel?"

"Sleeping like one," she looks to the house serenely.

"And the cherub?" he asks, pressing his head to her stomach.

"Listen."

They embrace. I look at the couple. Happy, even with all their paradoxes, happy.

"Did you tell him?" Kennedy asks.

I try to think what to say.

"I guess...here's to the future."

It comes out lamely, but Holden nods, satisfied. He starts to strum the guitar.

"This being Nashville, I will, of course, get to The King in a moment. But first, on this occasion..." He starts to play *Knockin' On Heaven's Door*.

Mama take this badge from me. I can't use it anymore. It's getting dark, too dark to see. Feels like I'm knockin' on Heaven's door.

The next morning, I drive away from the cabin as the McQueens wave me goodbye. I do not know when I will see him again. I do not know if I will see him again. My stomach feels empty and my throat hurts as I fake a smile, hug too long, and get in the car.

Still, Holden's word's echo, that loaded rendition of Bob Dylan's somber song.

Knock, knock, knockin' on Heaven's Door.

Through Tennessee, I drive up that old Southern highway. Just another speck on the road. Cars come and go, and nobody sees me.

Knock, knock, knockin' on Heaven's Door.

THE MAESTRO

The George Mason University Center for the Arts is a beautiful building. It looks something like an alien spaceship from the outside, a strange, aesthetically appealing placement of geometric arrangements you might call shapes, formed together in something beautiful. And from inside comes sweet music, in every sense of the word.

I walk into the grand, red concert hall where The Maestro, a hearty, hairy, lion of a man, addresses his class, which includes Winona.

He strolls around, observing the different musicians and adjusting them as he delivers his grand soliloquy.

"Cello." He points to the cellist who responds with some cello music.

"The magic flute." The flautist flutes.

Maestro reaches Winona as she grips her fiddle in anticipation.

"Hey diddle-diddle...time for the fiddle."

Winona caresses her strings with her bow, and the result is eloquent. I smile.

"You've heard The Song, no doubt. Because if you've heard one song, you've heard all songs, all songs being but a small significant portion of The Infinite Orchestra playing universally since time immemorial."

I walk in from the back. I quietly listen. I am not a musician, but I am a student, and I am curious.

"A symphony men and women can neither see nor understand but have nonetheless heard and appreciated their entire lives. For indeed they too are part of that music. What else could they be? Every fiddler, each singer, every aspect of the cosmos from the vibration of the quark to the humming of celestial bodies, contributes its own melodious tone to an overture greater than the sum of its infinite parts. And they are fiddling, fiddling, singing and rotating, and The Song remains the same and it never ends, it goes on and on and on, and the band plays on, in tune with the choir invisible, playing to the tune of The Conductor whose rhythm encompasses all of his children, for we are all players and love is his melody. Our village, people, is a symphony and we can't stop the music. Fiddlers, never cease your fiddling."

•　　•　　•　　•　　•

We walk along campus. She is holding my hand. Still, I contemplate.

"So. Maestro's pretty intense."

"Geniuses usually are. That goes double for the musical variety."

"Oh well, should we add you to that list?"

"I thought I was." She smirks, but then she sighs. Then she breathes in. She is bracing. "Ben, there's something I have to tell you."

Now I brace. I can sense the apprehension. I already have some idea.

"Yeah?"

"I got the scholarship."

She says it flatly. Matter of fact, because it is a fact, and that's what's the matter.

"Oh. Wow. Vienna. Uh…" I search, "Way to go!"

"Thanks. It's incredible. It's really something."

"I bet," I nod dutifully. This isn't easy for me, but I try to remain positive.

"A whole year abroad, that's…"

"About that." Winona's tone is soft but heavy.

"No, it's totally cool," I rush, not wanting to slow down to think. "You don't get long distance charges with Skype, we'll e-mail all the time. I might even be able to visit!" After thinking of my limited resources, I add, as a woeful afterthought, "once."

She sighs, and as the air comes out of her, I feel myself deflating.

"Ben…" She touches my arm, and I feel like a child. "These things don't work out."

"What-" My heart falls, from an immeasurable precipice, into the pit of my stomach. "What are you saying?"

"We have to be realistic."

"I'm thinking I would rather be fantastic!" I say this louder than I anticipate, but she tolerates it, which is even worse.

"We've had some great times together..." she begins a foregone conclusion in a tone so sorrowful, so detached, so condescending I want to scream.

"'We've had some-' What are you saying, 'We've had some great times together'?! Are you breaking up?"

"Call it a hiatus."

"I'll call it a dump, cause that's how you're making me feel! I mean, if you really wanted it to work, you could make it work." I state this emphatically. I know it to be true. "It's not just Vienna, is it?"

"It's..."

"Is..." I begin, but wary of other students about, I pull her to the side. Lower my voice. "Is this because I wouldn't- Because we never...?"

"No!" she snaps, before tilting her head and admitting, "Well...that and the other stuff."

"Cold. And I thought you weren't that kind of person."

"Ben," she begins, sharp, "I'm not leaving the country because you wouldn't fuck me. This is for the future of my academic career."

"So why not long distance?" I'm begging at this point.

"So why not join me?"

This takes me by surprise. And it hits me, and I see, briefly, what she means when she says this is so much more.

"What?"

"Take that leap." Her eyes light up with the possibility. "Come to Europe with me."

"Are you crazy? I can't just drop everything!"

"Yeah, maybe I am crazy," she returns to Earth, "but see, that's my point."

"That you're totally irrational and not making any sense?"

"Ben, again," she answers, annoyed, "it wasn't that you wouldn't fuck me- but yeah, that was a big disappointment. But it's what that represents. It's *why* you wouldn't fuck me."

She has to know the effect this is having on me. She's doing it on purpose.

"Would you stop saying that!"

"Why, does it scare you?" she answers scornfully. "You wouldn't FUCK me," extra malice in that word, "for the same reason you won't go to Europe." She calms herself. "I need something more. I need adventure. I'm suffocating, Ben. And I don't mean that about you. That was directed at Virginia. George Mason. All of it. I need to go somewhere else. I need to spread my wings. And if you can't be a part of that...It's your choice."

I'm welling up. It hurts to speak.

"Please don't do this."

Her voice is gentle, which makes it hurt all the more. I wish she was scornful again. I wish she was mean. There is nothing more brutal than this motherly affection as she rips my heart out.

"Look, it's a year abroad. Try new things. And when I get back...we'll see, okay?"

I don't respond. I can't even look her in the eye. She nods. She has her answer.

"Okay."

And then she kisses me on the cheek and walks away.

FATHER WEMBA

I'm finally back in Northern Virginia. It must have been a thousand years. I pull up to a drab cemetery at the edge of the county. Park my car and get out. This place is not frightening, but, which is worse, dull and forgotten.

I look at all the graves. So lonely. So foreboding. I can't do this yet.

.   .   .   .   .

I sit in the church. Solemn. Silent. Uncertain. It is a relatively new building, but the air is old and silent. My shoulders slump down in the pew. I'm the only one here. I could cease to exist. Nobody knows I was visiting.

Then a sound from the back as the door opens. I hear the priest's padded shoes on the soft carpet as he approaches.

"Hello," he says in a thick African accent. He is a young man, and happy to see me.

"Oh. Hi Father." I want to stand up, but I stay in place. "Good afternoon."

"I am glad to say, there is no funeral today."

"No." My voice drops, "But there was one about a year ago."

He sits down in the pew ahead of me. He looks back, arms on the pew, joining me.

"You are here visiting, yes?"

"Yeah, but I couldn't make it up the hill." I gesture to outside.

"It is kind of steep."

I mildly chuckle.

"No, that's not it."

"I know," he nods in understanding. "Someone important."

"He was. He was my professor."

"It is very important."

"He taught me so much, but...I don't even know what he's doing here. He believed some...crazy things at the end." I grimace. "And he killed himself."

The Priest nods slowly. Compassionately.

"This is difficult. But you know it is not our place to judge. God's mercy is infinite, and even suicides have a chance. There are mitigating factors."

"He was definitely not of sound mind."

"We don't know what happens next. But we can only pray."

"I do. And it's not, you know, *Hell*, I worry about. I think one of the most depressing things I can think of, is Heaven."

This surprises him.

"Heaven!"

"Well in Confirmation Class, they taught us that Heaven has layers. That we're not all equal. Even up there!"

"Yes, yes," he listens, thinking.

"My teacher said that the really good people get...I don't know, *more* Heaven? *Better* Heaven? And that I didn't understand, but I guess it makes sense, 'cause Mary's the Queen of Heaven, so we're all gonna be below her, so there's some ranking system. But it made me really sad. Cause when you're dead, that's it. That's eternity and there's nothing you can do to change. You're stuck. Maybe some serial killer who made a death bed conversion deserves less than Mother Teresa, but it's Heaven!"

He nods, getting it.

"Like I said, we don't get it. Heaven is the Beatific Vision. We all see God, but we don't see him yet. God's love is...*Agape*."

I sit up straight in recognition.

"Agape?"

"It's divine love."

"No, I get it! The Four Loves!"

We smile, sharing an acknowledgment.

"Yes! C.S. Lewis was very big at the seminary. Very celebrated. And Agape always has your best in mind."

"Works in mysterious ways."

"Yes. Let me tell you a story."

"Story time?"

"Story time! I was not always a priest, you know. When I was younger, I ran with the Area Boys."

"Like...boys in the area?" I don't know what he means.

"It's a gang," he corrects me. "In Lagos. We did petty things." He says this plainly, nonchalant, a sinner who casually recounts that from which he has been redeemed. "Sell drugs on the corner. Loot shops. Extort tourists. Boy stuff."

"Oh yeah. Sounds just like my childhood."

He smiles, knowing the gulf between us.

"Ha ha. But when I was 18...no longer a boy. They want me for bigger things. *Eyin*. The Teeth."

I can see it as he says it. His story, so different from my own, comes to life vividly in my mind.

• • • • • •

A sweltering apartment. It is a hot night in a hot city, but that is not why young Wemba is sweating. He sits on the couch across from Eyin, a fierce man with a shark's grin. Teeth. Flanking the gangster's throne are two big stern men whose faces betray little expressions.

"Eyin had a job for me."

Young Wemba shakes. He avoids Eyin's gaze.

"Maybe...Maybe there's another way," Wemba pleads.

"No. There is no other way. Little John pays."

One of the men hands Wemba a folded rag. He reluctantly takes it. He feels its weight. He knows what it is. And he unfolds it, sees the gun.

"In this way," Eyin insists in a voice that will not be questioned.

I take this in.

"He wanted you to kill a man?"

Father Wemba nods.

"Little John. Like in Robin Hood. He owed Eyin money, for drugs, and he wouldn't pay. So this was my chance to prove myself."

There is a huge line outside this bustling nightclub in Lagos. Wemba stands across the street, under a light, frightened.

Little John would spend the entire night at his club.

A limo pulls up. The bouncer opens the door, and Little John, fat and merry and unknowing of what's ahead, gets out, a prostitute on each arm.

Wemba watches and swallows.

I could find him in there.

He holds his stomach in pain.

•　　　•　　　•　　　•　　　•

Despite the weight of this situation, Father Wemba can look back with some levity.

"I was even more nervous than the night I got my cherry."

I look up. I know what he means.

"Great. Even you've done it."

He chuckles.

"It is not such a bad thing, for a young man to be a virgin. You are not married, no?"

"There was this one woman," I sigh, "I thought about it. But she's gone. Or, she's coming back, and...I don't know."

"We rarely do. Women are a mystery, my friend."

I don't want to get into this.

"So what happened? Did you..."

"No," he shakes his head, smiling, "God saved me. Do you know how?"

"How?"

"Ice cream."

•　　　•　　　•　　　•　　　•

Outside the nightclub, Wemba looks down at his stomach.

I had a pain in my stomach. I thought it was hunger. It was dread.

He takes a look at the nightclub.

I knew Little John would be there all night.

He turns and walks down the street, away from the club.

So I thought I'd have time to get something to eat. Kill the pain inside.

Wemba stands outside an ice cream shop, almost empty this time of night, but lit unnaturally bright. Wemba stands outside for a moment, almost hypnotized in awe by the humming fluorescent lights, the squeaky-clean white tile floors, and the colorful images of frozen dairy delights.

Or freeze it.

He enters. Brighter on the inside. He approaches the counter. Maria, the clerk, is angelic. She wears a cross.

"What would you like?"

Wemba is transfixed. He concentrates on her cross.

"What would you like?" she repeats.

"A Sundae. A Hot Fudge Sundae."

Then something occurs to him.

"No, two! I want TWO sundaes."

Wemba sits in the booth, eating his ice cream.

My mother never let me eat too much ice cream. But I was a man now. I was about to kill, so why not eat all I want?

Maria comes by to take one of his empty dishes.

"Do you want anything else?"

"Miss?" he asks, "how late are you open?"

"All night," she answers plainly. But to him this is a miracle.

"All night!"

"We're open 24 hours."

I had time, and no mother to stop me.

Father Wemba gets momentarily somber. He is thinking of his mother.

"She wasn't there to stop me from killing, so what difference would a little ice cream make?"

Wemba orders more and more ice cream. Shakes, cups, cones. His table is full and his stomach is fit to burst.

He leans back in his booth. Ice cream headache, stomachache, but a relived smile.

God always gives us a way out of temptation.

He groans.

I waited my time out with ice cream.

He drags himself out of the booth.

And I knew I could never kill.

Wemba gives a parting state back at Maria, before walking out of the store.

A quiet bridge, the loud Lagos night in the background. Wemba walks by the side of the water.

I was done in Lagos.

He stops, looks into the water of the Lagos Lagoon. He takes the gun out of his pants and looks at it.

I knew I could never come back.

He flings the gun into the lagoon.

And goes running into the night.

But I knew that God would show me a way.

Father Wemba finishes with a shrug.

"So here I am."

"That's a really cool story," I have to say. "Do you think he'll show me a way?"

"Maybe he already has."

•   •   •   •   •

Father Wemba stands outside the church, watching as I go into the cemetery.

I look back at him. He smiles. I nod.

I stand by Wilkinson's grave. Trying to think of what to say, because I can't say nothing.

"Well Professor," I begin weakly. "Here we are. Here you are...I'm not sure what to say. It's pretty hard. We didn't end on a good note. But what was it you told me?"

·   ·   ·   ·   ·

I sit in the front of the lecture center, grading papers

Professor Wilkinson comes in. He is in a merry mood.

"Benjamin!" he sings my name ebulliently. I look up. "How are the papers? Anyone cracked the secrets of the universe yet?"

"Well I'm getting a lot of funny answers."

He sits down.

"Splendid. G.K. Chesterton said that the riddles of God are more interesting than the answers of man. But you've got enough theories to go through. Maybe one of them will strike gold."

"And how are your own affairs?"

I am cautious but optimistic.

"Pretty good. Winona's just applied to a music program in Vienna, so she's pretty happy these days. Thinks she's got a great chance of making it."

"That'd be a year abroad," he points out, casually.

"I think we'd be able to work it out."

"And if not," he shrugs, "you'll still have the memories."

"Huh?"

He doesn't elucidate that supposed comfort. He picks up one of the papers.

"Oh my," he smiles, "The Predetermined Negative State of Human Nature: Let's Go Exploring with Calvin and Hobbes."

"Cute title, but it's pretty bleak. Ratt is essentially saying that we all suck and it was always meant to be."

"Why are so many young philosophers always so bleak?"

"Well..." I tread cautiously. "You encourage it, don't you? I mean, this class is about the extinction of sentient beings."

"I've expanded my own thought process recently. Nihilism is so...dull." He rolls the names in his mouth, bored, "Nietzsche, Camus, Sartre. When you get down to it, men of limited imagination. Many great thinkers make the illogical leap that if there is no Jehovah, there is nothing out there. But I look at the universe and see...if not some bearded man in the sky...something else. Maybe many other things. That's why these days I'm more drawn to Cosmicism."

"Cosmicism," I repeat. The word tastes dry in my mouth, and yet I sense some sense of ominous.

"Just look at the universe," he sweeps his arms, gesturing around. It is, after all, all about us. "As Sagan said, it's an awful waste of space. But why imagine extraterrestrials as little green men when they are just as likely to be elemental beings beyond our comprehension, more suited to the infinite they inhabit?"

This is beyond my own comprehension. I attempt to understand.

"So you think there are these...things out there."

He chuckles. He sees humor in this basic query, but he does not dismiss it.

"Well, I'm not about to get on my knees and offer a sacrifice to Cthulu, or even Shub-Niggurath, The Black Goat of the Woods with a Thousand Young. But the notion of such powers...it is interesting. Especially to think about taking it for oneself."

I feel an odd chill in the room. This is something entirely new and most definitely unwanted. He has not come from such a place before.

"I don't know what you're talking about," I start slowly, with all respect. "I think I preferred it when you were just talking about extinction."

"So, think about that," he shrugs, not in the least offended. "My previous lectures and published works are no less valid, no matter what path I end up taking. Dostoevsky, Freud, and our friend Nietzsche all had inglorious final days, but that doesn't negate anything they wrote before."

"The last word is not the only word." I appreciate it.

He smiles, musing. A warm man, with as much heart as ideas.

"You might as well pick and choose from the past, cause it's all gone anyway. Forget the bad, remember the good."

I am standing at this grave. I do remember.

"I guess that's what you meant about Winona," I tell him. "Whatever else happens, I'll always have the memories."

I cross myself and crouch down. I touch Wilkinson's grave. It feels coarse and gravelly under my fingers, but it is solid, and it is real, and I need that.

"I hope you found whatever it is you were looking for."

It sounds heavy in my throat, like an empty echo, and although those seem simply like the appropriate words to say, the sentiment is real, and I'm glad I said it.

I stand up and smile, because I feel like it.

"Here's to the good times, Professor. And there were a lot of them."

And it's true.

WINONA

I drive through Virginia, my mind a pool of quiet contemplation and loud thoughts. I hope that stopping by Wilkinson's grave, however briefly, was a profound experience, but it's too soon to tell. Maybe closure is a myth. But then, sometimes "it felt like the right thing to do" is more than just an obligation, catharsis or not. Maybe it wasn't for him.

Sitting next to me, crinkled, read, re-read, loved, hated, and ruminated on, is Winona's letter. She sent it across the world, from Vienna straight into my heart. I've lost count of how many times I've read it. Lunches where I can't taste the food and also sleepless nights. I've thought about throwing it away. I've thought about framing it. I've thought about burning it. I can do none of those things. Neither destroy it nor preserve it. It is a part of me, as is she.

Dear Ben...

Winona sits outside a cozy little café in Vienna. Café Mozart, I imagine. Like in *The Third Man*. She is wearing all black, I imagine. With a beret to complete the ensemble. She looks perfectly European, as she would want. It doesn't look pretentious or affected, or if it does, nobody cares. Of course, she is beautiful.

She is writing this letter by hand, so delicate the emotions and so committed she is. This will be no email. She wants this to be real.

Hey stranger. Remember me?

I am in my apartment, reading this letter for the first time. I stand in my kitchen, hand shaking. I read ardently, with a peculiar mix of disbelief, fear, bitterness, sadness, love, and other emotions. I didn't think I could feel so much and be so numb at the same time.

I did get your letters.

I am in my dorm room, drafting an email, my seventh since the last time I heard from her. I am nervous. The past six have gone unanswered, and my hope recedes the longer I wait.

And your emails.

The police are talking to Professor Skarsgaard outside the emergency room. I sit in the hall, texting on my phone frantically, in the hope of some solace on the other end. Despondent, desperate, tearful. Cold. Afraid.

Her voice cracks a little. She hesitates.

And your...texts.

She walks along the streets of Vienna. Alone. As I am. The towers dwarf her and her shadow looms large at night.

And I never responded.

I walk into my bedroom on another sleepless night. I am holding the letter.

I know, I'm a bitch.

I shake my head as a sit down, reading that line. I never thought that.

The University of Music and Performing Arts, Vienna. Winona approaches her new school. Her new life.

I guess I just wanted a clean break. I guess I thought that would help.

A new music room, a million miles away. Winona takes out her fiddle and starts again.

I wanted to move on.

•   •   •   •   •

I am driving through the Old Dominion, and as I get closer to campus, those same old sights start to look more familiar, and those same old feelings come rushing back.

I wanted us both to.

I think about our times together, as does she.

We had so many good times.

Her room in Vienna is small, but the view is immaculate. She unpacks, eager to start living. She stops when she comes across the photo of her and I at Cox Farms. We had that framed. Now, it gives her pause, and not in a good way.

But I thought that chapter was over.

I am at George Mason. I have been gone for so long and so much has changed, most of all myself. I park my car, student turned stranger turned me, and get out, ready to try again, or at least I tell myself.

And you can't go back.

Bright-eyed and optimistic, Winona explores Vienna. Its sights. Its sounds. Its smells. Yes, in that bakery in which she will write this letter wafts the smell of fresh delights to her. She cannot resist. It is a new place. It is a new her.

Vienna has been very good to me.

Winona climbs the Alps. She comes to a rest, sitting on a jutting rock, grass below, snow above, the world before her. She is breathless, in more ways than one.

I've seen another world.

At the Vienna Conservatory, Winona gets her big solo on stage.

I've played my song in the Infinite Orchestra.

. . . . .

After the show, in a quaint Viennese pub, Winona sits at a table with some of her new friends, laughing and talking. She is comfortable. She is happy. She is home.

I've made new friends.

From across the table, Gustav, tall, dark, and handsome, catches Winona's eye. She smiles.

. . . . .

He walks her home through the streets of Vienna. The night air is crisp and full of possibility.

I even fell in love.

More assertive than me, Gustav pulls Winona in and kisses her.

My heart sinks when I read this. I fall onto my bed and my chest hurts too much to weep.

Winona and Gustav.

Exploring the streets of Vienna.

Hiking through the Alps.

Making music together.

Living.

Loving.

Or I...thought I did.

At the Erdberger Bridge, Winona and Gustav secure a love lock.

But you can't keep the past locked away.

Winona throws the key off the bridge.

Not forever.

Gustav kisses her.

No matter how hard you try.

I walk across campus. Has it really been so long? Am I really here again?

It's funny the way things work out- or don't, really.

Winona hugs Gustav, a parting motion.

I don't know.

Gustav gets on his bike. Winona watches him speed away, out of her life.

Maybe he just wasn't you.

In her Vienna room, Winona stares up at her ceiling, pensive.

You know, you really got me thinking, Ben. All the things I remembered about you.

I am in the lecture center, speaking in front of the class. I am not even aware of what Winona loves.

The way your voice would go ever so slightly British when you spoke in front of the class.

We are at Danny's Bar. Winona slides the beer to me. I am surprised. I take the cold perspiring beverage, brushing her warm fingers in the process.

The first time our hands touched.

I am in the library. I am swamped. I sit at a desk, surrounded by a stack of philosophy books.

All your books of wisdom, hoping you could find the secrets of the universe.

Winona sits down across from me. I look up and smile, relieved.

We are in the hayride at Cox Farms. I put my arm around her.

How you let me into your past.

We sit under a tree on campus, relaxing in the shade and looking at Tie-Breaker in amusement.

How much you loved my silly little drawings.

Michael is another college douchebag with a guitar he can't play, but we are in his room, and we have to listen. Lori, Aiyshah, Winona, and I in the audience. A joint of marijuana is being passed around.

Winona takes a drag and offers it to me.

I wave my hand.

I admired your innocence.

She passes the joint to Aiyshah and leans her head on me.

You made me feel like a good person.

We are at the pumpkin patch. I help Trevor pick out his future jack-o-lantern. Winona watches, admiringly.

Because you are a good person.

We are in Professor Skarsgård's living room. I have just said something toast-worthy. Professor Skarsgård raises his glass.

Winona smiles. She squeezes my hand. I notice.

And you were with me.

I smile at her.

And, well...

I stand outside the registrar's office. It is time to begin again.

I just hope you know how much I appreciated that.

I am in the registrar's office. I turn in my papers to Mrs. Dumblaskas. I doubt she remembers me, and in truth she is little more than a face and a voice to me. But there are no supporting characters in real life. Everyone is the star of their own story.

Being near you.

We walk back to Winona's aunt's house.

I cherish everything we did together.

I sit on a bench at George Mason, reading her letter. My papers are filed. Class starts next week. All I have in the present is the past.

All of it.

We are in Winona's room on that fateful night. She takes off her shirt.

Even the parts that scared you.

I am scared, but I am also in love, and in this moment, maybe they're the same thing.

Maybe those were the most important parts.

She makes her case for this night. She begs me. She appeals to every part of me.

And I'm not going to apologize, because there's nothing to apologize for.

I kiss her on the cheek. Awkwardly. I leave.

I think I get it. Now.

She watches me go.

I still don't agree with your reasons.

I walk out of the house, burning with shame and desire and love and regret.

But I get it.

She looks out her window and sees me out under the street light, cold and retreating. Her light is off. I don't know she's looking.

Ben...

Her eyes water up.

I love you so much.

I am at the hospital, sitting in a chair too weak to hold my pain. I cradle my head. I am a wreck.

And I am so sorry.

It is a cold autumn day at Café Mozart. Winona sits alone.

A thousand times I thought about calling.

She looks at her phone. Hesitates. Puts it down.

Or writing.

•   •   •   •   •

The Vienna Cathedral is an ancient building, as beautiful as it is immense. Right now, it is quiet. Winona sits alone.

Or something.

She sits on her bed, uncertain, as I am. As we all are, so often.

I didn't say anything, because what could I say?

I am in my dorm room. I know his blood isn't on me, but I can't get it off. I lie curled on my side, in the fetal position.

I wanted to be there for you.

Suddenly, she is at my side, holding me.

I wanted to let you know that everything was going to be all right.

I trace my hands over her face.

But I wasn't there.

She vanishes, like a ghost, and I am alone again.

And that's my only regret.

I am at George Mason, now my school again. I finish writing a text. After waiting a moment, I send it.

I hope you've moved on.

I am in therapy.

I am in Los Angeles.

I am on the road.

I am at George Mason. Professor Skarsgård sees me from across the way.

I hope you're with people you love.

I am with my father.

I am with Stacey.

I am with Holden.

Professor Skarsgård and I embrace. In this moment, we don't need words.

And who love you back.

We walk across campus, renewed. Ready to start again. Not where we left off, but somewhere new.

Because you deserve it. If anyone does, you do.

• • • • •

Winona finishes writing her painful letter at the café. At this point, she's not even sure if it will ever be read. But she needs to put it out.

Well, I just wanted to say...life takes us strange places, you know? Mine's taking me back home, end of my program, end of next month.

It's only natural to come here. The history of the universe is also our own history, and this museum will always be in my heart. Our first date. The first time she made me feel more like the person I am now.

I see her from afar. I approach.

Yours, Always...

I reach her. I am afraid to reach out, but it is beyond time for fear. She turns around.

Winona.

She looks different. Europe has changed her. Older, wise, with a hint of mature melancholy. She's happy to see me, even with the weight between us.

"Hi," I don't stutter, and I don't hesitate. More will come later.

"Hi."

We search for words. It's quiet, awkward. There so much to be said and so little which could suffice.

"You look good," I say truthfully, trying to take her all in.

"So do you."

"Europe's been..."

"Yeah, it really has," she finishes.

"I'm glad to see you," I say it simply, honestly, and that's enough.

"Me too," she answers, and that too is enough.

• • • • •

We walk through the museum. Tracing the steps of the universe and our own lives together.

All my life, people have been telling me the meaning of life.

We come to a crossroads. Several directions we could go down.

My memories are in fragments. I play them back and forth, but not in order, like a CD of life's greatest hits that keeps skipping around.

We come to the giant timeline. An appropriate place, for all the reasons.

Maybe you just got to go back to the beginning, try to sort it out. But maybe it's not that easy.

She traces her fingers on the timeline, eons in an instant.

We come to the preserved extinct.

Maybe nobody knows.

Mother, who tells me the simplest truths about God a child will ever need to know. The last word is not the only word, and no matter what happened next, I'll always have that.

The Priest. A simple prayer that lasts a lifetime.

Mr. Todd. His cats a metaphor for something grander than kindergartners could comprehend, though we will always remember.

Scout Master. An oath summarizing all that matters.

Mrs. Marley. A day that echoes throughout a life. A harsh summarization, but not untrue.

Professor Wilkinson. A man of a madness and mystery. I may never understand him. I may never want to. But he will always be a part of me.

Dad. In some ways as damaged as me. All the world's a sea, he sees, and when he takes me on his boat, he shows me not to crash.

Nina. I don't know how much I get out of yoga beyond pure relaxation and the simple, moving mantra, "May all beings be happy and peaceful."

Trent. He is right. There are some assumptions you can't make about people, no matter how much you'd like to. But sometimes the best is true.

Holden. Warrior poet. Maybe he talks more than he listens, but he's worth it. A soldier of principles. A friend unafraid to tell you what you don't want to hear. A husband and father. Discipline. Love. Semper Fi.

Chris. The Serenader of Dreamland. When you don't have the words, there's always music.

Jason Lee. Sometimes there is insight even in vulgarity.

Wilson. A Christian driver. Helping hand. Not all who wander are lost, and sometimes God's road is bigger than you're ready for, but just keep on driving on.

Stacey. Like Holden, she tells me some hard things I don't always want to hear. But she comes from a place of love. This has become a family of islands, but I thank God we've got boats, that when we reach out to each other, none of it is lost.

Nelson, who doesn't count his chickens on the wrong side of the river.

Dr. Modine, who is smart enough to study the brain but wise enough to admit he cannot know the mind. Sometimes the most important thing to know, perhaps, is to accept when we don't know.

Professor Skarsgård. The kindest teacher I have, and always there when compassion is more welcome than any answer could be.

Father Wemba, who tells me God always shows us a way, as unlikely as it looks, in as strange a place as it may be. Salvation, revealed through ice cream.

Me.

Her.

We come up with all these explanations and philosophies, but sometimes I think it's all a lot of noise we make up, because we really don't know anything.

We come to the Prehistoric Woman, still so far gone.

And we're all so scared.

She leans on me.

· · · · ·

I talk to Winona as we walk outside this significant place, able to tell her, at last, my thoughts.

"But I thank God, I thank him every day, that I have the chance to ask these questions. And that I have people to make the whole thing less scary."

She looks up. She likes that.

"Yeah."

"I may never know the 'meaning of life', whatever that means. But I know what I want in mine."

She looks at the street corner. That's where it all started. Where we started.

I take her hand.

"Hey."

She looks at me in the eye. A pure, knowing gaze. She sees me and I see her, and she hears me, and that, at long last, is enough.

"Do you mind if I love you?"

THE END

NOTE FROM THE AUTHOR

Word-of-mouth is crucial for any author to succeed. If you enjoyed the book, please leave a review online—anywhere you are able. Even if it's just a sentence or two. It would make all the difference and would be very much appreciated.

Thanks!
Brian

ABOUT THE AUTHOR

Brian Carmody is the author of *Hellish Beasts* and the award-winning screenwriting of *The Batting Cage* and *Aunt*. A natural romantic, he is still searching for the meaning(s) of life. He currently roams in Southern California.

Thank you so much for reading one of our **Coming of Age** novels.
If you enjoyed our book, please check out our recommendation
for your next great read!

The Five Wishes of Mr. Murray McBride by Joe Siple

2018 Maxy Award "Book of the Year"
"A sweet...tale of human connection...
will feel familiar to fans of Hallmark movies."
-KIRKUS REVIEWS

"An emotional story that will leave readers meditating on the
life-saving magic of kindness."
-Indie Reader

www.ingramcontent.com/pod-product-compliance
Lightning Source LLC
Chambersburg PA
CBHW011138100726
47898CB00009B/3030